PWNED

by
Matt Vancil

Quiet Thunder Productions, Inc.
Seattle, Washington
USA

Published by Quiet Thunder Productions, Inc., Seattle, WA, USA

Edited by Rachel Edidin
Copy Edited by Janie Dullard

Cover Art by Rob Carlos
Book Design & Layout by Sherry Lynne Baker

Project Management by Kevin K° Wiley

Printed and bound in the United States of America

Publisher's Cataloging-in-Publication

Vancil, Matt

PWNED / Matt Vancil ; [edit. Rachel Edidin & Janie Dullard]

Summary: A fictional novel about a man reluctantly entering the world of
MMORPGs to recover his lost love.

p.cm.

Paperback ISBN 978-0-9909097-0-5
Hardcover ISBN 978-0-9909097-1-2

Acknowledgements

Many thanks to everyone who made this possible:

The PWNED Development Team—James Snyder, Elaine Simone, James Herbert, Hawke Robinson, Robert Schimmel, and Steve Payne—for enduring the early drafts, and for your input and optimism;

Rachel Edidin, for honing the manuscript and helping me get out of my own way; Janie Dullard, for catching all my typos; Rob Carlos, Crystal Frasier, and Sam O'Hara, for bringing the world to life; K° Wiley, for keeping the gears turning; Two Bards (Andy Dopieralski and Scott C. Brown), for making the pitch look good;

James Youngman, for giving the manuscript the game designer stamp of approval; Stuart Hume, for giving it the Aussie gamer stamp of approval; Tony Becerra, for not stabbing me (yet);

Zombie Orpheus Entertainment, Andrew Obertas, Douggie Sharpe, and Greg & Nancy Vancil, for your support;

Judith & Garfield Reeves-Stevens, my writing godparents, who told me that writing a novel was a when, not an if;

John Frank Rosenblum and Cindi Rice, for your years in the trenches;

All my backers and fans, for your trust and patience; And Camille and Wesley, for everything.

for Dad, my first storyteller, editor, and fan

PWNED

Prologue

Lorki splintered the helmet of the last automaton with his seven-foot sword. The mechanical monster wheezed like a punctured bellows and collapsed in a heap of clockwork.

Lorki looked around, his blood drumming. Destroyed automatons littered the dungeon's five-way intersection. He smelled machine oil and blood soaking into centuries of dust. No more enemies.

He shook his head to clear it, and the red haze of battle faded. Two of his team's five members lay dead in the sand: the archer and wizard. He'd never bothered learning their names.

Lorki snorted. Weaklings, flinging death from a distance. Contemptible, really. True warriors met their foes face to face.

Only the healer, the indifferent assassin, and Lorki himself were still standing. Their fate was in the healer's hands now.

"You're hurt?" the healer asked. Lorki pointed to the dead. The healer nodded, began to cast a revival spell over the fallen archer. Lorki was hurt, yes, but taking the brunt of the damage was his job: holding enemies at bay while his weaker comrades whittled away at them from the flanks. He pulled a healing potion out of his gladiator's harness and downed it, bottle and all.

They'd come in fifty strong, an elite band of warriors honed to deadly precision over years of adventuring. They were an unstoppable army—until the automatons had scattered their ranks.

He couldn't remember when he'd last seen another unit, and all he could hear down the distant tunnels was the clanking and clacking of the tomb's guardians.

Doubt, that most dangerous of foes, crept in. There was no sunlight down here, no way to tell how much time had passed since they'd gone down the cold gray steps. Time stood still when Lorki was lost in the rage of battle, but judging by the damage to his equipment and the healer's dwindling supplies, they'd been in this labyrinth for the better part of the day, and no end was in sight.

The archer gasped and convulsed, snatched back from death. The healer paused to rest before turning to the fallen wizard.

Lorki had died before. He didn't care for it, but you did what you had to do—and trusted the healer to bring you back. So long as they had a healer, they had a chance.

But a chance for what? Lorki wasn't even sure what they were searching for—the legend was vague. Some artifact from the dawn of time, a weapon that for centuries had eluded the brightest and bravest. Lorki grinned around his tusks. If his were the hand to claim it, those bastards in—

The archer shouted a warning. A trio of automatons had rounded a corner and was surging towards them—spinning gears, shrill whistles, whirling blades.

"Protect the healer!" Lorki roared, and hurled himself at the machines. The red rage took him.

He heard his ancestors sing as he cleaved through the first metal man's shield. He would hold this ground to his death and beyond. He took a slash across the face and returned it, spraying bolts across the intersection and drawing the attention of another automaton.

"Shield!" he yelled to the healer. She began casting.

Lorki heard a shriek, and the top half of the archer landed at his feet. He snarled. *Weaklings.*

Another scream, and the assassin fell dead. *The hell is this?* Lorki thought. It was almost like they had no healing support.

The final automaton zipped over the assassin's body and slammed into Lorki, knocking him into the far wall. He roared and sprung back to his feet.

"Shield!" he bellowed again. What was the fucking healer doing? His tanking drew crazy aggro, and there was no way he could hold three without her.

Lorki saw her where he'd last seen her—waving her arms above her head, still casting the spell that should be shielding him, repeating the same action over and over again. That spell had a casting time of seconds. The only reason her animation would be looping was if...

The healer froze—and disappeared.

The three automatons converged on Lorki. They were gonna wipe.

"Shit!" yelled Lorki. It come out "@#$%!" because he had the parental controls activated—sometimes he let his daughter play on his account.

Opening Cinematic: Human

The Age of Men is nearing its end.

After years of war against the savage Nations of Chaos, only a single human state endures: the proud kingdom of Marrowstone.

The last beacon of civilization in a dying world, the Men of Marrowstone and their allies in the Kingdoms of Order—the noble Elves, stalwart Dwarves, wise Dryads, and mysterious Ord—remain united against those who would destroy them.

The Age of Men is nearing its end... but a new age, an age undetermined, has just begun. Go now, and take your place among the great heroes of old!

> **Pick a server type:**
> - **Balanced (mix of RP and PvP)**
> - **RP (role-playing)**
> - **PvP (player vs player; not recommended for new players)**

1

Anniversary

TIP: You can add important guild events to your in-game calendar!

"You can do this." Reid kept his voice down, even though he was pretty sure Astrid couldn't hear him. His heart beat like a rabbit's as he fastened the brittle cuffs on a dress shirt he'd inherited from his grandfather and wiped the sweat from his temples.

Reid found Astrid where he always did: hunched over her computer, plugged into her game. He turned the ring box around and around in his pocket. *I should just spin her around. Spin her around, look her right in the eyes and say it: I've loved you since you made me cool, and I want to spend the rest of my life with you.*

He knew why he didn't. He was afraid she'd push him away and spin right back to the game. So he just stood there, sweating in his grandfather's suit, twiddling his grandmother's ring in his pocket.

She must have sensed him there after a time. Or maybe her guild was taking a pee break. In either case, she turned around, and Reid's breath caught in his throat.

Astrid was the kind of pretty that punches you in the gut and locks your knees, and makes you instinctively glance at the third finger of her left hand. Slim with curves, a millennial Bettie Page in faded red highlights and yoga pants.

Astrid smiled at him, pulled one of her headphones away from her ear.

Reid swallowed. *Now's my chance.* "Hey—"

"Why are you sweating?"

Reid wiped a hand across his forehead. "Oh. Big day at work." *What am I doing?*

"Oh."

"You sleep all right?"

"My hip's been bothering me."

"Sorry." *Maybe if you weren't in that chair all the time, it wouldn't hurt so often,* he didn't say. "Are you hungry? I could go for some breakfast."

"Uh… sure, thanks."

Reid regrouped as he sliced strawberries over oatmeal. *Come on, you can do this. Just get it out. What is with this sweating? I look like I ran a marathon.* He changed into a fresh shirt and brought Astrid breakfast. "Maybe you'll get in a nap today."

"Who can sleep?" she said. "No rest for the wickeds. We're doing an epic dungeon today, fifty-man endgame. Been planning it a month. Damn lucky I don't have anything else going on."

Reid forced a smile. "That's cool." It would sting if she'd forgotten. "Did you get those job links I sent you? You're way qualified. Think you'll apply?"

She shrugged. "I've got a job."

Reid bristled. "Could you clean up a bit, then? The laundry needs folding and the sink's a superfund site."

Astrid swallowed the last of her cereal. "Day's full already. Have a good day at work. I don't know how you do it, day in, day out. Why are you all dressed up?"

The wind went out of Reid's sails. She *had* forgotten. "No reason."

She snapped her fingers, nodded. "Right — big day at work."

"Yeah, something like that."

"Okay, well... happy accounting." She spun back to the computer. "Punch Lodge in the throat for me." She pulled the headphones back on.

The ring box weighed heavy in his hand. *You can still do this.* He squeezed the box to keep from shouting. *Get it out.* "So, Astrid. I was thinking... we've been together a long time now, and we're already *living* together, and doing other, you know... spousey things, so I thought maybe we could make today more..."

He chanced a look up at her. Her eyes were locked on the screen. She hadn't heard any of it.

"Official." He let go of the ring box in his pocket. "Happy anniversary."

Reid had done what he could to personalize his cubicle. He still considered it his cell in corporate purgatory. The main decoration he'd put up was a poster of wine and cheese pairings, with color-coded thumbtacks to indicate which he'd tried, which he'd liked, and which were next.

Reid was sticking a picture of himself and Astrid at the beach to his work computer when Lodge ducked into his cubicle.

"Douche-hammer," said Lodge, by way of greeting.

"Turd-burgler," answered Reid. They exchanged a complex handshake and chest bump.

Lodge was a technical writer from fifth floor. He and Reid had started the same week and hit it off at the employee orientation; they'd been lunch and break buddies ever since.

The first time Reid's boss had seen Lodge, he'd been plugging in Reid's monitor after helping move furniture during the latest desk shuffle. Reid's boss had assumed Lodge was an I.T. guy. Lodge never corrected him, as it gave him a free pass to visit Reid on eighth as long as he poked a few keys.

"Check it out," said Lodge. "Game night. Tonight, my place, dudes only. Cheap beer and store brand chips for everyone." He leaned down and whispered conspiratorially, "If it sounds too good to be true, it is. There will be no chips. Also, you're gonna erase your hard drive if you keep doing that."

"With fridge magnets? Is that your official I.T. Guy diagnosis?" The handbook prohibited tape or glue on company property, so he had attached a photo of Astrid to his monitor with a pair of magnets, cutesy cartoon mice dancing on oversized wheels of cheese.

"You would put these on a fridge? Where people could see them?" Lodge inspected one of the mice. "Where do you even get these?"

"This creamery in Oregon. I dragged Astrid out last year." Reid mimed speech for the boy mouse: "We can see how all my favorite cheeses are made!"

And the girl mouse: "That's the single most lamest thing ever!"

"I agree with Girl Mouse," said Lodge. "So. Game Night. Should I save you a spot?"

"Sorry," said Reid. "Can't make it tonight."

"I've got plans," said Boy Mouse.

"Big plans," said Girl Mouse.

"Please stop doing that," said Lodge.

"Never!" said Boy Mouse. "Give to me kisses, sexy mouse!"

"Make me a woman, cheese-breath!" Reid made the magnets kiss, with appropriate smooching sounds.

His boss naturally chose that moment to appear. "Reid," he said. "What does the manual say about toys?"

Reid froze. This was exactly how he'd lost his Captain Cotswold action figure. "Magnets," said Reid. "Mr. Habermann. Sir. They're actually magnets."

Habermann nodded. "So they are. And what does the manual say about toys?"

Reid recited from memory. "Employees are allowed knick-knacks in the workplace as long as they're not a distraction."

"And if a member of the Board happened by, and saw you playing with those?" Habermann held out a meaty hand. "I'd say they've become a distraction."

"But." Reid looked to Lodge for help. Lodge flattened his smile—*sorry, man.* "But they're mementos."

"I'm sure you'll remember them fondly." Habermann beckoned. Reid meekly handed them over. Boy and Girl Mouse vanished, doomed to continue their carnal encounter in the breast pocket of Habermann's designer suit. "Can't have you distracted right now. Not until the Englebrook-Meyer account's done."

Reid nodded, repeated "Engelbrook-Meyer" to cover that he had no idea what that was.

Habermann looked around his desk. "I don't see it being done."

"Englebrook-Meyer?" Stalling, Reid glanced around his desk. An email had just arrived in his inbox. "Is that the one I just got?"

Habermann sighed. "And it isn't being done, because...?"

Reid checked the send time. Five minutes ago. "I just got it."

"When you were playing with your toys." It wasn't a question. Habermann shook his head slowly. "The Board appreciates initiative, Reid. Back on track. Focus on your goals." He finally seemed to notice Lodge. "Is there somewhere you need to be?"

Lodge unplugged Reid's printer with a flick of his foot. "As soon as I get the printer running."

"Okay, then." With nothing else to confiscate or dress down, Habermann sauntered back towards his corner office.

Lodge waited until Habermann's door clicked shut. "Douche. Sorry about the magnets. Hey, about tonight—I'll keep a spot for you at the table."

"For I am the Elijah of game night. It's not gonna happen."

"Well, if it does. If it turns out Astrid's, you know... occupied."

"Occupied?" asked Reid.

Lodge moaned like a zombie and mimed some zombie-typing.

"It's not that bad."

"Has she noticed you live together?"

"Oh, she's noticed."

"Good," said Lodge. "That's the first step. Keep your distance, at least initially. First, acclimate yourself to her habitat, get her used to your presence, and only then initiate contact. It's amazing what we can learn from these strange, magnificent creatures."

"Addicts?"

"Women."

✤ ✤ ✤

Reid returned to the apartment with a picnic basket in one hand and a bouquet of flowers in the other. "Man return to cave!" he yelled, striking a man pose, which he held with increasing discomfort as he waited for a reply. "Babe?"

He padded into the apartment. The blinds were still pulled, the laundry hamper still loaded and lying by the door where he'd left it. "I'm gonna go out on a limb, say you didn't get around to cleaning."

He found Astrid at her computer, where he had left her that morning. She was still in her pajamas.

"Hey. How was your day?" He knew she wouldn't hear him with the headphones on, but he kept talking anyway. "Mine? Oh, you know, the usual emotional gratification I get from helping multinationals cheat on their taxes. Thanks for asking."

She didn't even look up.

Reid went on. "Had to kill a nun with an ironing board at the bus stop. *Again.* Got blood and nun juice all over my shirt. And then I got to check receipts for the next ten hours *and* skip lunch. But I'll tell you this—it's all worth it when I have this to come home to."

Still no response. Reid pulled a headphone off one ear, let it snap back.

She whirled, startled, and smiled that perfect smile. "Boo-Bear! I didn't hear you come in."

"Couldn't tell." Her smile wiped away all the frustration, and he grinned back.

She kissed him. Angels sang, and the world went away. Astrid adjusted her headphones so one ear was free and turned back to the computer.

Reid glanced at the screen. Astrid was steering her character through a dungeon, some enormous underground complex, but numbers and icons and status bars utterly obscured the scenery. "How's the raid going?"

"We've been in this ass-damn maze for twelve hours!"

"Mm. Productive day."

"Had to kill a bunch of kook raiders camping the instance, too."

"I'll take your word for it."

"And one of them actually rolls a smuggler toon so he could yell at us for ganking him. Hey, dumbass? It's a PVP server. You want to play with the big dogs, raid some T-9 gear or go home and play Puzzle Pirates."

"So that's a no on those job links."

"I *have* a job. I finished the newsletter while we were rezzing. I'm almost done."

"So you've mentioned," said Reid. "When was it? Oh, right. Every day for the last two years." He dropped the flowers on the desk in front of her.

She looked from the flowers to the card in his hand with a semi-panicked *"shit, what am I forgetting?"* expression. "Is that for me?"

Reid handed it over with a nod.

Astrid opened the card and concert tickets fell out. "Oh, my God. The Proclaimers!"

"Yes. But! Not till after dinner." He whipped the blanket off the picnic basket with a flourish. "I stopped by Hess on the way home. Got some gouda and stilton, some imported muenster, brie, three kinds of bread I won't bore you with… let's see, black currant marmalade, that salami you like, this weird German meat-paste in a squeeze tube—I don't know, the lady

14

said it was good, and if you can't trust Germans… Anyway, if we leave now, we can make Point Defiance by sunset." He set the basket aside, took her hands in his. "Picture it. Just you, me, questionable German tube meat, and Scottish heartland rock. No work. No video games. Happy anniversary."

Astrid smiled at him. The panic was still there.

"The Shot," he explained. "Seven years today."

"Oh, my God. No, it can't be." Astrid checked the date on her phone. "Holy shit, you're right."

"Yeah." Reid beamed. He couldn't help himself. "It seemed like a day worth remembering."

She giggled. "I remember."

"Damn right." He took her hands. "Look, I'm… sorry I've been riding you so hard about the game and the job thing."

She nodded. "Look, I know it wasn't the plan, but I'm paying my share of the rent—"

"I can be better," he said. "It's just, today means a *lot* to me, you know, and the game—"

She sighed. "Yeah."

"I don't know what I'd do without you. The best part of my life is what I've spent with you." *Despite the game*, he didn't say.

She looked down. "Oh, Boo-Bear."

Got her.

"I don't get why you're so good to me sometimes."

"Easy. I love you."

"I forgot it was today."

"That's okay."

"I didn't get you anything."

"You didn't have to. But you still can." She eyed him curiously. Worriedly? Nah. "I was hoping we could make this anniversary more official."

Astrid arched an eyebrow. Reid dug the ring box out of his pocket and got down on one knee.

Astrid's hands flew to her face. "Oh, fuck."

"Astrid," said Reid. "Will you — ?"

The kiss nearly knocked him over. Astrid came up for air and ripped off her headphones and glasses. "Shut up."

Reid broke free. "Is that a yes?"

"I said shut up."

The next kiss did knock him down. She slipped into his lap and kissed him again. Reid raised a fist in triumph as she groped for his belt.

A tinny scream in the distance made Astrid sit bolt upright.

"What?" gasped Reid. "Why'd we stop?"

Astrid's headphones had pulled loose. Now sounds of battle were coming from the computer. Combat filled the screen and swirled around Astrid's character, who was standing stock still.

Reid's heart sank. "Don't. Please."

"Sorry." She looked at him with her please-forgive-me face. "I have to finish here."

"You have to finish *there*?"

"You don't understand." She pulled her t-shirt back down. "I can't just abandon my group."

"But you can abandon me?"

"It's not like I'm going anywhere!" She slammed herself down in the chair and pulled on her headset.

Reid zipped back up. "Yeah, so I gather."

She sighed. "I am *so* almost done with this."

Reid grabbed a dry erase marker and wrote "Dinner @ 6" on her monitor. She erased it with her hand without taking her eyes off the screen.

Some time later, Reid set a plate of bread and cheeses by Astrid. She mumbled a thank-you and ate one-handed, never once looking up from the computer.

Reid checked the time on the concert tickets—8:00pm, one night only. He checked his watch. 8:35pm.

Lodge answered the knock at his door, and flinched when he saw Reid's face. "Dude."

"Hey." Reid halfheartedly went through the motions of their handshake. The concluding chest bump was decidedly morose.

"You okay?"

"Is there still a spot at the table?"

Lodge nodded.

Reid held up the picnic basket. "Cotswold?"

2
Game Night

TIP: Enable "Call to Adventure" to see available quests!

Reid slumped behind a forest of empty beer bottles. Beyond, small wooden knights faced off across a colorful cardboard battlefield.

"So she looks over the side, right?" Reid said. "And she says, 'This is where I'm building it. The world's first extreme bed and breakfast.' And then she base jumps while giving me the finger."

"And what did you say?" asked Leo, brushing crumbs out of his beard and onto his bowling shirt. He took a bite of some cheese roughly the color of a traffic cone.

"I was too busy not terror-puking to say anything," said Reid. "But when we got back to the trail head, I pointed out that the cliffside wasn't exactly zoned for business. Also that parking would be hell."

"Still don't care," said Cass. He'd remained laser-focused on the gameboard the entire time Reid had been talking, totally ignoring the bounty of cheeses and bread.

"Anyway, so she starts drawing up a business plan—her

folks are in real estate so she knows this shit, right?—and she actually gets commitments from a couple of travel agencies, so it looks like it's gonna happen! How awesome cool is that?"

"On a scale of one to shut up?" said Cass. "The latter."

Lodge spun listlessly in his desk chair. "Would you make a move already?"

"Patience," said Cass. "Your asses can't all get kicked at once. Or maybe they can." He placed his pieces, only to snatch them away with a last second frown.

"She started planning it out," said Reid. "I was gonna join her, like 'Hey, and I can do a wine and cheese shop in the place,' and she wasn't really sold on it, but, you know—it was *our thing*. But that was before." His head slid to the table. "She hasn't even talked about it for months. Not since the game."

"You're not still paying for that shit, are you?" asked Leo.

"I never was," said Reid. "It's her hobby." She paid for the game and her half of the bills herself. She'd worked for her parents' real estate agency part time—website, and a little IT— since college. It paid well but was meant to be a temporary thing while she got her passion project up and running. Now all that extra time just went into the game. She could still knock out their newsletter in about eight hours a week, which let her ignore Reid's calls to get a better job, or at least get out of the apartment.

"I thought you didn't want to talk about it," said Cass. "*For the last three hours.*"

"I've lost her."

"Yeah, sounds like."

Reid flopped his chin on his folded arms. "Not even to a real person. To a game! She's online all the time with her *guild*, playing make believe."

"Here." Cass offered Reid a ninth beer. "Put some shut-up juice where those words are coming out."

"Thank you." Reid swigged.

"Okay." Leo brushed off his bowling shirt. "Let me see if I get this. Your girlfriend—your mega-hot girlfriend, the one with the pixie tattoo—"

"Gelfling," Reid said between gulps.

"*Gelfling* tattoo—is a gamer. And you have a problem with this."

"No! It's just that it's all she ever does!" *It's because the game's more important than me.* He drowned the thought in beer, then planted the bottle in the forest of empties. "It's like I'm not even there."

"Then dump her," said Cass. "That's what I'd do."

"Same," said Leo.

Reid scoffed. That wasn't an option. Not even. "You don't drop your partner just because you're going through a rough patch." *A two-year rough patch...* But still, they were living together. Practically married. He was *lucky* to be with her. She was *way* out of his league. He'd never find anyone like her again.

Reid looked to Lodge for support. Lodge was married. He understood.

"I'm with them," said Lodge. "If we're being honest."

Stung, Reid gestured for a tenth beer.

Cass's eyes locked onto a section of the board, and he grinned. "There we go." He slammed his knights down. "Boom. Flip your tokens, scrubs."

Reid flipped his tokens with numb fingers, not really paying attention.

Leo nudged Reid and pointed to the board. "You do realize you're attacking a vastly superior force? That's kind of suicide."

Reid hadn't noticed and didn't care. "Blaze of glory and all that." He took another swig.

"Maybe you want to reconsider—" said Lodge.

"Nope!" said Cass. "Orders are final once flipped. Bring it on, Light Brigade! You're about to Crimea River."

Leo glared at him. Cass smiled back and enunciated carefully. "Cry-me-a-river?" Leo studied the game board. "Get it? 'Cause back in the 1840s—"

"1854," said Leo. "And wait." He eyed the board, nodded decisively. "Okay. I'm supporting Reid."

"What?" puffed Cass. "No, you're not. Why would you suck like this? Is this about my awesome Crimean War joke?"

"Partly. If you go down, it'll open up my flank."

"I'm not going down!"

"Whoa, you totally are." Lodge finished a quick scan of the board. "I see it now. Hell, yeah. I'm with Reid, too."

Reid grinned. It was nice to have people on his side, even if he didn't quite know why.

Cass glowered. "Mutineers! Deserters! I have more force on the board than all of you! As Melville said: 'With dice and justice, I smite at thee!'"

Leo shook his head with a sigh. "Not even close."

Cass hurled a handful of six-siders across the table. They bounced off the game box and scattered. "Well, dick in a cake."

"Ha," said Leo. "You got pwned."

"By a noob," added Lodge.

Cass folded his arms and sulked. "I most certainly did *not*. There was asskickery, yes, but no pwnage."

Reid looked to Lodge. "There's a difference?"

Lodge grinned. "Pwn, verb: to overwhelmingly defeat, usually in humiliating fashion. Used in game to taunt opponents and rub in victories."

"So, like… Germany-France, World War II?"

"More like Spaniards-Aztecs, 16th century," said Lodge.

"No," said Leo. "Mongol invasion of Khwarezmid Empire, 1219-21. Total pwnage. Not unlike the sort you unleashed on our friend here."

"Or maybe," said Cass, "like your gamer girlfriend and you."

Reid sank into himself. Cass looked pleased, until Reid's first sob worked its way free.

"Oh, shit," said Cass. "No, don't do that. No crying. If you cry, then *I'm* the asshole."

Reid ground his eyes shut. That tenth beer was a mistake. "I don't know what I'd do about her." He'd meant to say "without." Shit, he really *was* crying now. "I can't lose her."

Leo actually looked befuddled. "Why not?"

Because I'll die, Reid didn't say. It's what happened to the men in his family when they lost their wives, whether it was to death (his grandpa) or realizing what an unredeemable shit you were (Dad). Well, maybe Dad wasn't *dead*, exactly, but it wasn't like he—

Cass slammed his hands on the table, toppling the beer bottle forest and startling everyone. "You wanna know what to do? Apparently I'm the only one who's been listening and cares, because it's *obvious* to me." He pointed across the table dead between Reid's eyes. "If the game is what's come between you, then—pow!—*you get rid of the game!*"

Reid blinked. Sat up. "You think so?"

Cass spread his hands, the picture of innocence. "Would I steer you wrong?"

Leo opened his mouth, and Cass slapped a hand over it. "Be a man, Reid. Go home, right now, and confront her. *Right now.*"

Lodge frowned. "I'm not sure that's the best idea—"

23

"Silence, naysayers! Ride that wave, cowboy!" Cass yelled. "Ride it home! Right now! While you've still got the nerve!"

The asshole was making sense. "Yes," said Reid, nodding, pointing at Cass. "You see this? *This* is what I need to hear."

"You go, Reid!" said Cass.

"I'm gonna do it!" Reid jumped to his feet and missed. Leo helped him up off the carpet and aimed him towards the front door.

Lodge snatched Reid's keys out of the goblet on the mantle. "I'll drive you." The door slapped shut behind them.

"Nice kid," said Leo.

"Girl's probably asleep anyway." Cass spun in his chair to face the game board. "Well, would you look at that! He left before his turn was over! Which I believe, according to the rules, invalidates that *entire* last battle."

"You're a dick."

"A dick who's gonna win." Cass reached for the dice.

Reid padded into the apartment and draped his blazer over the back of the recliner. Astrid was where he'd left her, still playing, still in her pajamas, her face awash in the light of the monitor.

Any other night, Reid would have just stood there and waited for her to notice him before he skulked off to bed. Tonight, the thought of going to bed by himself pissed him off. The ring box lying forgotten on the floor pissed him off more.

Reid dropped his keys onto her desk from a yard up. The jangle scared a jump out of her. "Jesus, Boo-Bear!"

"It's tomorrow."

"I'm almost done."

"You said that…" Reid checked his watch. "Eight hours

ago. And the day before that. And last week, last month. There are *tablets* in the *pyramids* with you saying that."

Astrid sniffed at him. "Are you drunk?"

"Pshaw." Reid dismissed that with a wave. He leaned towards the bookcase and missed. "Ow."

Alarmed, Astrid half-rose from her chair. "Are you okay?"

He saw her then, a brief glimpse of the Astrid he had fallen for—that wide-eyed girl who'd kissed him under the piano at Jonah's aunt's house. She was worried about him, and that should have been some comfort, but this time it just hurt.

"I'm sorry, Reid. I know you're unhappy." Her hands on the keyboard, she looked at the screen and sighed. "We're just spinning our wheels, aren't we?"

Reid grunted. Admission was the first step to recovery. "Could you maybe help me up?"

The screen flashed and changed. Astrid went rigid. "My God," she said. His piano girl was gone. "There he is."

Her back was to him again. He tried to escape from under the bookcase, couldn't. "Um. Help?"

"Fuck me, I'm so close."

"What the *hell*, Astrid?"

She shot him a brief look, a guilty look. "I'm sorry, Reid. I really am. This isn't who or where I thought I'd... well. I'm working on it."

She pulled her headphones back on and spun back to the computer.

Reid's dam burst. He dragged himself up the bookcase, tearing the cuff of his grandfather's shirt. "God *damn* it!"

Still wobbling, Reid stormed to the kitchen, ripped open a drawer, and pulled out a pair of scissors.

Astrid glanced away from the screen. "What are you doing?"

Reid grabbed her Ethernet cable. "Something I should have a *long* time ago."

Astrid went pale. "Reid, *no!*"

He sliced the cord.

The action on Astrid's monitor froze and kicked back to the login screen, where a message popped up: *You have been disconnected*. Astrid stared at Reid like he'd just clubbed a seal pup.

"Okay," said Reid, "we're gonna talk."

Astrid burst past him, nearly knocking him back into the bookcase. She yanked open the hall closet and rooted frantically through bins. "Oh God, oh no, oh *God*..."

"This has gone on long enough."

"You're fucking God damn right it has."

Reid picked his way through the clutter towards her. "I really think we--no, *you*, it's totally you—have a problem. Sorry, that was accusatory. Let me rephrase."

Astrid hurled a plastic crate against the far wall. It exploded in a shower of office supplies. With a triumphant cry, she pulled a fresh cable from the mess and darted back to the computer.

"You play *all the time*," Reid said, stumbling back towards the desk. "I can't remember the last time you *weren't* plugged in to that thing—"

"Come on!" Astrid yelled. She connected the replacement cable and threw herself back into the chair. "Come on, come on!" She spammed the *enter* button on the login screen. "Comeoncomeon*comeon!*"

"And that makes me feel a little bit—shocker!—unimportant. Like you don't even care I'm here."

Astrid jerked and let out a choked cry. The screen was littered with corpses. Reid could finally make out the dungeon's gray sand beneath glowing letters: *You have died*.

Astrid slowly spun her chair to face Reid. Her face was

expressionless. "This? Is the *one thing* that keeps me going."

Reid held out the scissors at arm's length. "Pwned." He mic-dropped them, stumbled into the bedroom, and passed out.

The alarm jackhammered through Reid's ears and started drilling into his brain.

Reid cracked his eyes open and immediately regretted it. He was never going to drink anything again, he decided, including water.

"Astrid!" he croaked. She must not have heard him. The alarm kept screaming. She had to have heard that at least.

He noticed he was still wearing his suit. He must have forgotten to change. He'd do that later, after a handful of asprin and a week of sleep. He ripped the alarm clock out of the wall.

In blessed silence, Reid laid on his side on the sweet, cold bed, and slowly panted the rest of his way awake.

"Astrid," he said again. He tried to swallow, but someone had glued his throat shut. "I could really use some water." It wasn't going to be a good day. He was already breaking his no-drinking pledge.

Astrid still hadn't replied. She must be really mad at him. At least she was wearing the headphones so he didn't have to listen to the damn game.

He noticed her side of the bed was still made. She'd never come to bed. But the drawers of her dresser seem to have been pulled out.

Reid scanned the room. Her backpack was missing from the top of her dresser. In the closet, the hangers hung bare. Reid hoped for a moment that maybe they had been robbed, but once he got to the living room, the evidence was unavoidable:

Astrid's computer was gone, and so was she.

Lodge just stared at him, one hand cupped over the receiver of his desk phone. "And you just came to work today?"

Reid quivered. "I didn't know what else to do."

"I'll have to call you back," Lodge said into the phone.

Reid let Lodge steer him to the tiny office break room and pour him a cup of office coffee. "You've checked with her friends?"

Reid's blazer was draped around his shoulders like a blanket on a shipwreck survivor. "They're not speaking to me."

"Parents?"

"She doesn't tell them anything. My *God*. She *left* me. She actually *left* me over *that*."

"Wow. Well, you know, I—" started Lodge, and then caught himself. Reid prompted him to continue. "You know what? I'm gonna say it. *Good*. *Finally*. Rip off the band-aid. I mean, I figured it'd be *you* getting fed up and leaving *her*, but hey, the effect's the same, right? This has needed to happen for a while now. Good for you, I mean it. And good riddance."

"Lodge—"

Lodge held up a hand. "Don't. No. Not this time. Consider this a retroactive intervention."

"Lodge—"

"*No!* Dude, this is what you need. This is *good*, Reid."

"I asked her to marry me."

Lodge winced, grunted. Stared at the floor. "Oh, fuck. I'm sorry, man. Scratch what I said. I'm invoking Man Code, and shall forever hold my peace."

Reid regarded him evenly. "Forever?"

"At least until you come to your senses and I can deliver an appropriate *I told you so*."

"I can fix this," said Reid. "It's my fault. I overreacted."

"I'm sorry, *you* overreacted? I heard that correctly?"

"I can fix this," Reid repeated. "If I could just talk to her, explain. I know I could make this all right."

"It doesn't exactly sound like she wants to be talked to."

"You're supposed to be helping me."

"Okay, fine. Do you have any idea, any notion where she might have gone?"

Reid crushed the styrofoam cup and threw it towards the garbage, missing by a yard. "All I know is that wherever she is, she's still playing that damn game."

"Not much to go on," said Lodge.

Reid didn't hear him. "That's it." Why didn't he think of it sooner? He grinned triumphantly at Lodge. "She's still playing the game."

Wizards and warriors battled across the cover of *Fartherall Online*. *Over 10 Million Players Wolrldwide!* it boasted. *1,200 Hours of Content!*

Reid did some quick mental math. If he put in eight hours a day and talked to a hundred players an hour, it would only take him thirty-four years to find Astrid. *Lose Yourself in Adventure!*

He fought down a surge of panic. She had to be in the game. Someone in there had to know her.

He set his laptop on Astrid's desk. While the game installed, he opened the two-liter he'd picked up at the store and dug through his cabinets until he found a bag of not-quite-stale tortilla chips. The computer chimed when the installation finished. Reid double-clicked the *Fartherall Online* icon.

A robot cowboy appeared on screen. It tipped its mechanical Stetson with an emotionless "Boy, Howdy," and reclined against the logo for Boy Howdy Games.

That graphic dissolved into a massive gate flanked by torch-es, *Fartherall Online* inlaid in gold and jewels across the wrought iron.

With a click of the mouse, the gates swung wide onto a character creation screen. Reid clicked the first two options he saw: "human" and "rogue." With a triumphant clash of cymbals, Reid's human rogue appeared on screen, all dashing and rakish.

The game prompted him for a name.

Reid drummed his fingers. He couldn't use his real name, ob-viously. She'd see him coming, and if she were still mad—which she was sure to be—he'd never get within hollering distance.

Maybe something to remind her of home? He looked around the living room for inspiration: the patch of white on the wall where her monitor had kept the sun from bleaching the paint, the unused concert tickets on the floor. "Boo-Bear," she had said, not 24 hours ago, "I don't get why you're so good to me."

Reid spun in his chair. "You want a name? Meet Boo-Bear." He typed it in, hit enter.

A message popped up on the screen: *That name is taken.*

Reid blinked. Someone else was running around the game with the pet name Astrid had given *him*. With a snarl, he tried Boobare.

That name is taken.

Bewbear.

That name is taken.

Boob-air.

That name is taken.

"Oh, come on." He didn't have time for this. He chucked caution out the window and typed in "Reid."

That name is taken.

"Of course it is."

He tried Brokenheart. *That name is taken.* Brokenlove. *That name is taken.* Brokenliver. *That name is taken.*

"You're shitting me." What alcoholic gamer had already taken that name? He glared at the box. *Over 10 Million Players!* it reminded him.

Cheese Man. *That name is taken.* CheeZeus. *That name is taken.* Lord of Citrus. *That name is taken.* Flapjack Wendy. *That name is taken.* 3.14159. *That name is taken.*

He tried That Name Is Taken. That name was taken.

"This game sucks." He typed it in. "This. Game. Sucks." *That name is taken.*

Reid roared and slumped. He'd drunk half of the two-liter already, and he wasn't even through the front door. He'd be the first player in history to lose at a game without even logging in. He could almost see Astrid watching over his shoulder, shaking her head in disbelief. "Jesus, Boo-Bear, you're embarrassing me. You're such a friggin'—"

"Noob." Reid tried it. It wasn't taken.

A portrait of Noob, stalwart human rogue, appeared on screen.

Reid perked up. "Well, all right then."

A prompt appeared: *Begin Adventure?* He hit *Yes.*

The character creation screen gave way to a bird's eye view of an architecturally impossible fortress of steel and glass. Heroic music swelled and sank into a melancholy lament sung in some forgotten language by an invisible choir.

"The Age of Men is nearing its end," intoned a morose narrator. *"After years of war against the savage Nations of Chaos, only a single human state endures: the proud kingdom of Marrowstone.*

"The—"

Reid clicked *Skip.*

3
Making Enemies

TIP: Joining a group increases your chance of survival!

Noob faded into existence in a field of flowers, with "Noob" hovering alongside "Level 1" above his head. *Great*, thought Reid. *Way to advertise your mediocrity.* He looked around Noob's new digital world.

Noob was standing in front of some redbrick monastery. On the grass beside the building's chapel, a crowd of characters were jumping and dancing in their underwear. Some he recognized as elves and dwarves of standard fantasy fare, although the blue-skinned people and the tree folk were new. Each had a name and level floating above their head, but there were so many bodies knotted together that it was hard to get a read on any one.

Rings of stones with runes carved into them lay scattered, seemingly at random. Higher-level characters in cartoonishly excessive armor were squaring off in each ring, smashing each other with oversized weapons and blasts of magic.

"Hi," typed Reid to no one in particular. No one in particular said anything. "Is Astrid here?"

Fireballs burst against armor. Bloody swords rose and fell. Naked elves cha-cha'd. It was like he wasn't even there.

"Does anyone know Astrid Wheeler?" Nobody replied.

A pair of guards was patrolling the monastery's interior. Maybe they'd know where to start looking. Noob headed in that direction—

"CHUCK NORRIIIIIIIISS!"

—and a dwarf in a neon cowboy hat bowled him over. The dwarf ran up to the naked partiers, whipped a keg out of nowhere, and exploded in a cloud of beer foam and beard trimmings. The partiers cheered.

Noob scooped himself out of the sudsy blast zone and fled into the chapel. He found the guards stiffly walking their rounds. They weren't trying to kill each other, and both were fully clothed, so Reid figured the computer must be controlling them.

He followed the guards into the chapel's sanctuary. Before the altar stood a knight with a glowing scroll floating above his head.

Noob marched up to him. "Hey, there. Hi."

The knight ignored him.

"I'm looking for someone."

No response. He didn't even move.

"I was wondering if you could help me."

The knight remained steadfast in not talking.

Noob waved a hand in front of his face. "Hello? Bueller?" Nothing. He looked around. "Did this guy stroke out or something?"

A wizard in garishly sequined robes stopped to laugh and point. The name above his head proclaimed him to be Fyreballz, Level 1oo "Noobtard! Dumbass here thinks he can talk to a bot!" He laughed. Frills and feathers heaved. "OMG lolz, fucknut!"

Reid wasn't about to take crap from a man dressed as a Mardi Gras float. "Yes, ha ha. Let's mock the new guy. Imposing dress you've got there, Sir Prance-a-lot. Does Tinkerbell know you stole her curtains?"

Fyreballz stopped laughing. "This, dumbsuck," he said, indicating his cascading ruffles, "is the raiment of the Arch-Lich Necorpsur! The rarest boss drop in the Moonhollow! It is *not* a dress!"

"Neat. Does it come in men's?"

Trumpets blared. A ring of the rune stones fell into place around them. *"Fyreballz has challenged you to a duel!"* boomed a voice from the heavens.

Reid blinked. "What?"

Fyreballz held out his palms, crackling with eldritch fire. "We duel, bitch! Choke on my hetero man-fire!"

Noob ducked out of the circle of stones and behind the knight. "I'd like to request sanctuary. Can I do that? If that's okay, say nothing."

He hadn't noticed the blue-skinned woman in the corner until she spoke. "Aw, that's so dumb it's almost cute." She stepped between Noob and Fyreballz, turned to the wizard. "Scram, squishy. The green's with me."

Fyreballz glared at the newcomer. "This don't concern you."

"Does now."

"I'm just finishing what he started!"

"Oh, I see," she said. "*He* started it. A Level 1 challenged a geared-out 100. In a Level 1 starting zone." She turned to Noob. "You didn't, did you? You're not *that* dumb, right?"

"I might have commented on his dress."

"It's a *raiment!*" Rage-fire erupted from Fyreballz's shoulders. "He offended my honor! I demand recompense!"

She unslung her bow and stepped into the circle of stones. "Dude? It's a dress."

From behind the knight, Reid could see her name: Yanker, Level 100. Beneath that, he could make out another name, this one bracketed in chevrons: <Pwny Xpress>.

Fyreballz was apparently sizing up the blue archer, too. "Whatevs." The flames around his hands vanished in puffs of smoke. "I shall wreak my vengeance another time, Noob. And never forget—you're all gay!" He made a rude gesture and ran backwards out of the sanctuary, his robe bouncing jauntily.

"Gay!" he reiterated from the narthex. "All of you! *All* gay! Gaytards!"

"You can come out now," Yanker told Noob. "And by the way? Stepping out of the circle doesn't cancel the duel. Major rookie mistake."

Noob emerged from behind the knight. "Thanks. Dunno what that guy's problem was."

"Gay!" Fyreballz hooted from the distance.

"NP. Can't stand that crap." She kicked a runestone out of place, and the rest of the ring disappeared. "Stupid griefers get bored and have to ruin the game for everyone else."

Noob took his first good look at her. She was pretty as far as bald Smurf-skinned women went: slightly taller than Noob, with a swimmer's build and golden eyes. Her lime and lavender armor resembled a scaly speed skater's uniform. On her tabard was a mounted knight, middle finger heroically extended.

"Your armor is cool."

"Thanks," she said. "Had to kill the Aurora Dragon like sixty times to collect all the bits."

Noob nodded, not understanding.

Yanker threw her arm around the unresponsive knight. "So, guy here who won't talk to you? Right-click him."

Reid did. The scroll above his head vanished as the knight pounded a mailed fist into his palm. "These blasted orcs!" he said. "Every year they grow bolder!"

Noob blinked. "I'm... sorry to hear that. But I guess that happens. Anyway, I was hoping you could help me —"

"The Skullspear tribe has taken up residence in the mines outside Marrowstone! From there, they raid our villages and kill our people!"

"That can't play well in the papers."

"This will not be tolerated! The time to strike is now!"

Noob looked at Yanker. "Is it?" She shrugged.

"They shall bathe in the blood of our vengeance! Go forth, rogue! Slay ten Skullspear orcs and bring me the head of the orc chief Dromor."

"Uh..." Noob did a quick scan of the room. "You've got like a dozen Level 105 knights in here not doing anything. Why don't you send them?"

"Return in triumph, and you may choose your reward!" The knight held out his hands. Above his palms appeared a pair of copper pieces and a bowl of fruit.

"Sweet," said Noob. "I was just thinking how what would really get me through this black pit of despair is some pineapple."

"I'll bet it's a *gay* pineapple!" yelled Fyreballz from off-screen. "*Gay*, like you!"

The rewards had disappeared, and the knight had gone inert again. Reid zoomed in on the knight's face. "Hello? Angry knight guy? Was that it?"

"First time in, I take it?" asked Yanker. Noob nodded. "Try

clicking again."

The quest giver roused. "Well, Noob? Have you brought me the head of Dromor?"

"Yeah, I ran right out and got it without breaking eye contact."

"That's all they're programmed for," said Yanker. "They can't give complex answers."

Noob turned to her. "Could you help me, then? I'm looking for someone."

"Yeah, kinda gathered. What's the name?"

"Astrid. Astrid Wheeler."

"Yeah… no. What's her toon's name?" Noob stared at her. "Really? Her *character*, kid. What's her character's name?"

Reid blanched. "I…" All the glimpses he'd caught of her playing, all the times she'd made him look over her shoulder while she did something cool, and he never thought to look for the name above her head. "I don't know."

"I'll bet it's a *gay* name!"

Yanker drew and fired a bomb-tipped arrow into the ceiling of the narthex. The resulting explosion flung guards and bits of guards in all directions and buried the hallway in rubble. The surviving guards continued along their courses, unmoved by or oblivious to the fate of their comrades.

A guard arm landed at Noob's feet. "The guards…"

"Will respawn in a few." Yanker re-slung her bow over her shoulder. "As, unfortunately, will Fyreballz. Anyhoo, the person you're looking for? If you don't know her name —"

"I do!"

"Her *handle*, I'd say you're pretty well screwed."

"But she plays all the time!" The bodies of the guards had begun to fade. "I mean, someone here *has* to know her! Right?"

"Dude, she might not even be on this server."

Reid felt a distant sinking sensation. "Are there *many* servers?"

"Last I checked? About three hundred." Reid's stomach dropped through the floor.

The rubble blocking the entrance to the sanctuary had faded away. Yanker saluted him with a "Cheers, lover," and bounded out past the newly resurrected guards.

Noob darted out of the monastery. Through the chaos of dueling 100s and naked dancers, he spotted Yanker heading toward a primeval forest bordering the monastery grounds. "Hold up!" He ran after her. "Wait, please!"

Yanker stopped, turned. "Really? What?"

"Look, please—help me."

"More?"

"I don't even want to be playing, okay? I hate this game."

"And this is supposed to sway me?"

"I just need to get in touch with her, that's all. Or someone who knows her. Is there like anyone in-game with account holder information? Subscriber names, contact info, that sort of thing?"

Yanker considered. A pair of nude elves ran by, on fire. "Admins. They monitor gameplay in the most populated zones. Kind of like lifeguards, except they'll let you die."

"Admins, got it. Where can I find one?"

"Marrowstone City." She pointed toward the tangled forest. "Other side of Inkwood and the Moonhollow."

"Thanks." Noob bowed and ran for the woods.

"Whoa! Don't go *in* there, you dumbjack!"

"No time!" he called over his shoulder. "She's already been

gone a day, and I have to—"

A streak of white. A globe-headed arrow slammed into the ground at his feet in a burst of coagulant. Noob jerked to a stop, ankle-deep in glue. Yanker circled around in front of him.

"As I was saying," she said, shouldering her bow, "you're heading towards a level capped zone, an *epic* zone. It's absolute death in there. Too many beasties. And it's way heavy in PVP."

"Like the plastic?" More burning elves ran by.

"Player versus player. In there, you're fair game. Especially with that name. Seriously, what were you thinking? Was 'Kill Me' taken?"

"Probably. I didn't try that one."

She narrowed her eyes. "Are you griefing me? 'Cause if you're griefing me, I will gank you and camp your arse, just you wait."

Noob shook his head. "I don't even know what those words mean."

"Okay, then. If you want to get to Marrowstone, go back to the starting zone, level out, and walk around Inkwood like everyone else. The quest chain will lead you right there. It won't take you more than a day or so. Just play the game."

"I don't *want* to play this game! I'm not here by choice! I've got a life I'm trying to get back. Could you just take me through the woods, just to the city?"

She looked away. "I've got plans."

"You're playing a video game."

"Somehow? Still not swaying me."

"Look, I'm sorry. You've been very patient with me. It's— I'm not having a good day. I hurt someone I love, and I can't get in touch with her, I'm seriously worried about her, and—" He looked up. "And now a bunch of naked elves are throwing squirrels at me." A barrage of rodents rained down. The elves cheered. "It's obvious I don't belong here."

"Ya think?"

"But if you do this *one thing* for me—get me to the city— you'll *never* see me again. I promise."

"Tempting." Yanker brushed a disoriented squirrel off her shoulder. "What the hell. I'm out of dailies anyway." She pulled Noob out of the glue trap. "Stay close, try not to die."

"Stay on the path." Yanker set out at a steady jog down the dirt trail that snaked between the gargantuan trees. Goblins darted through the trunks around them but stayed clear of the road. "It's just a few minutes through here."

"Cool," said Noob. "I'm hoping to be off in an hour."

"An hour. That's cute."

Noob craned his neck to take in the canopy. Hundreds of feet above, the highest limbs interwove in to a latticework that kept the forest in preternatural darkness. A gust of wind, and a flurry of leaves swirled down, each trailing its own pattern. "These graphics are amazing."

"Yeah, it's pretty sweet. Have you seen the stills from the expansion?"

"They're making more of this?"

"They should be. It's a brilliant world."

Far off the road ahead, in a shadowy section of the woods, a wall of gnarled, up-reaching trees ringed a wide hollow. It looked for the world like a temple complex with wooden walls and towers. "What's that?"

"The Moonhollow. Super tough dungeon. Don't even think about—*stay on the path!*"

Noob had missed a turn and run a few yards into the wood.

He corrected his course back to the trail. "Sorry," he said, jogging back to her. "That didn't seem so bad."

A giggling goblin bounced out of the woods and stabbed Noob in the face. A red bar appeared above Noob's head and shrunk by ninety percent. "Hey!"

Yanker stopped. "What?"

"That guy stabbed me!"

A single arrow from Yanker dropped the goblin. "I said *stay on the path*. What part of that was hard to understand?"

"He just ran up and shanked me!"

"Well, yeah. You aggro'd him."

"I didn't even know he was there!"

"It's triggered by proximity. And because your level's so low, their range is gonna be like doubled."

Noob's health bar crept back up to full.

"That"—she kicked the dead goblin—"is why you stick to a level-appropriate zone and don't go play in—"

Another goblin jumped on Noob's back and stabbed his health bar to a sliver.

"Oh, for fuck's sake."

"Um... help?"

Her arrow took the goblin above the eye. Noob watched it twitch at his feet while his health spooled back up.

"What do I do?"

"First, get back on the damn fucking path." Noob did. "Second, when you're getting smacked, don't just stand there. You've got a weapon. *Do* something. Run, drop a defense, whatever. Did you even do the tutorial?"

"I think it's pretty clear I did not."

Yanker sighed. Chuckled. "Okay." She looked around. "All right. See that squirrel?"

"Yeah."

"Kill it."

The squirrel wiggled its nose at Noob. "Uh… no thanks?"

"Look, it's the only thing in these woods that won't drop you in two hits. It doesn't even have levels. It's here for decoration."

"Then why do you want me to kill it?"

"I don't *care* if you kill it or not. But you need to know how to defend yourself so I won't feel bad about dumping your arse in the big bad woods. Now stab me some squirrel."

"Okay, sure." Noob glanced down at his victim. "Sorry, Nutkin." *I am Noob, Slayer of Squirrels, Scourge of Small Cute Woodland Creatures.* Reid hit some keys at random.

Noob reached out, whip quick, and touched the squirrel. He heard a plunk, and an acorn appeared in his inventory. "What was that?"

"That," said Yanker, "was Pickpocket. A useful ability, sure, but not in the middle of combat. Try again."

Reid hit more buttons. Noob burst into dance, rolling his hips with carnal enthusiasm and disco pointing skyward. "Why am I dancing?"

"No idea. That's not even a button."

"How much damage am I doing?"

"To the squirrel? Or my patience? Just right-click it."

Click. Noob drew a dagger he didn't know he had and stabbed the squirrel. Its health bar appeared and shrank by three-fourths. With a squeal, the squirrel fled into the woods.

"Yeah!" yelled Noob. "Not too shabby. That wasn't so hard." Noob disco-pointed and hip-rolled in triumph. "Why am I still dancing?"

The wounded squirrel ran right into a crowd of goblins. As one, they turned, spotted Noob, and bounded towards him in a cascade of giggles.

Yanker unslung her bow with a sigh. "I got them, but you owe me for the arrows."

"Thanks."

Yanker took aim.

A dash of movement caught Noob's eye. He spun, saw a white-cloaked character with a crystalline staff a stone's throw away. The name was *R-something*... he didn't catch the full thing before she ducked behind a tree.

"Hey," said Noob. "There's someone—"

"Busy," said Yanker.

Noob spotted another figure, this one translucent—charcoal-skinned, chalk-haired, with ears that pointed past the crown of his head—sneaking up behind Yanker. "Who's that?"

She shot two goblins dead at once. *"Busy."*

"There's someone behind you."

The dark elf plunged his sword into Yanker's back. Yanker's health bar appeared and dropped by half. "Lurker bastard!" She whirled on the now fully visible dark elf and went for her sword.

The elf became fully visible, as did his name—Greef, Level 100, of <Something Wicked>. He disarmed Yanker with a flick of the wrist.

"Run for the city!" she cried, "West-northwest!"

"What's happening?"

Greef stabbed Yanker in the throat. With a scream, Yanker toppled forward and died.

Greef flicked the blood from his blade and sheathed his sword. On his tabard, a big spiky monster dangled a squirming victim above its mouth.

Noob, still dancing, drew back. With a laugh, Greef pointed behind Noob.

Noob heard a goblin giggle. He turned right as the wave of goblins crashed over him, stabbing gleefully.

Reid slumped back in his chair. On the monitor, Noob lay dead in the forest, face down beneath a message: *You have died.*

Well, that hadn't taken long. Reid considered how much time it might take to make a new character and find another untaken name, and the thought made him want to puke. He hadn't factored mortality into his Astrid-finding calculations. He wondered what the body count record for a single player was, and how quickly he'd break it.

On screen, Greef squatted up and down over Noob's head, electronically teabagging him.

A new message popped up beneath the first: *Go to the Underworld?"*

Why the hell not? Reid clicked *Yes.*

Noob materialized in a cavern so thick with mist he could barely see his hand in front of his face. He was a ghost, wispy and incorporeal, his body made of the same mists of the cavern.

The mists parted before him, and Noob found himself standing at what could only have been the Gates of Hell; the moaning faces encased in the iron were a dead giveaway. The Grim Reaper scrutinized him from a podium by the gates.

"It is not yet your time," intoned the Reaper. "Return to the world, and live again."

Noob didn't move. The Reaper pointed a bony finger. Where he pointed, a light shone through the mist and burned a passage through the fog.

Ghost-Noob jogged down the mist-shrouded tunnel, away from the Reaper and the wailing gate.

❈ ❈ ❈

Still in ghost form, Noob emerged from the Underworld into the woods where he'd died. A creaking sound made him look behind him just as the misty tunnel popped out of existence.

Noob walked to his corpse, which prompted another message on Reid's screen: *Resurrect here?* Reid clicked *Yes.*

Mist poured from Noob's body. A bell pealed, and Noob was flesh once again. He knelt by Yanker's body. "Hey… are you okay?" It seemed an odd question to ask a corpse. She didn't respond. Maybe she hadn't found her way out of the Underworld. Maybe that was only a thing for low-level characters, and the stakes were higher when you were higher level. Maybe it actually *was* her time, and the Reaper had drawn her through the Gates. In which case, he'd literally gotten her killed.

"Sorry," he said. "I'm really sorry. Thanks for being nice to me. And patient. And, uh… good luck in Hell, I guess. For what it's worth." Her body faded and was gone.

Someone cleared his throat. Noob rose to find Greef smiling at him.

The dark elf pointed at Noob's level and said something that came out in gibberish.

Noob considered running. Greef's blades were sheathed at his hips. That seemed promising. Reid couldn't imagine there being any in-game benefit for killing a character 99 levels below you. And it *had* been the goblins that had dropped him before, not Greef.

Greef said something else in gibberish. Noob figured he'd try diplomacy.

"Hi—"

Greef cut him in half.

* * *

Noob re-materialized before the Gates. The Reaper glowered down at him. "It is not yet your time."

"Are you sure about that? Sure feels like my time."

"Return to the world, and live again." The Reaper pointed down the tunnel through the mists.

Ghost-Noob considered his options as he watched Greef dance obscenely above his bisected corpse. If he reanimated, Greef would kill him again. He could log out and wait for Greef to get bored waiting to kill him and leave, but that was time not spent looking for Astrid. He could always make another character, but that toon would be stuck back at the monastery, and he'd have to play for hours to get to Marrowstone. God knew he'd never find someone else to take him through the Deadlyfuck Murderwoods.

Reid figured he could make it about ten steps before Greef hacked him to death, in which case he'd at least be ten steps closer to Marrowstone and an Admin. He sighed, resigned. If it got him closer to Astrid, he was up for a few hundred rounds of catch-me-kill-me.

Angels sang, mist poured from his body, and a newly reincarnated Noob sprinted west-northwest and made it two whole steps before Greef threw a net that anchored him in place.

The dark elf sauntered over. Pieces of his armor disappeared with each step until he was naked but for a loincloth.

Greef decked Noob across the face, knocking his health bar to a sliver. "How is this fair?" Noob asked. The second punch took his head off.

"Hey, is it yet my time? I'll bet it's my time."

"It is not yet your time."

"Righto."

Last fucking time, thought Reid, *and then I'm logging out, burning my laptop, and joining a monastery. Preferably one with a vow of silence.* The celibacy wouldn't be a problem. It wasn't like he was ever going to have sex again anyway.

He found Greef running back and forth between Noob's head and body, teabagging one after the other. *This*, thought Reid, *this is pwning. I get it now.*

Reid positioned Noob's ghost at the maximum distance the *Resurrect here?* prompt would allow, which put a good twenty yards between him and the dark elf slapping balls on his face. With a *click* from Reid, Noob took flesh and took off.

After three paces, he was still alive. He chanced a look back. He'd gotten the jump on Greef—the dark elf had just now noticed he'd slipped away and was chasing him in a dead sprint. *I'm gonna make it!* he thought, and was so intent on watching Greef that he didn't notice the goblin mob until he'd run right through them.

The goblins cheered and joined the chase, all giggles. Noob bore down and sprinted. *West-northwest, west-northwest, west-northwest —*

—and the woods parted onto a golden plain. Beyond, the mighty computer-generated fortress of Marrowstone City shimmered into resolution. Noob made it to within a stone's throw of the wall before Greef punched him in the back of the head.

The punch stunned Noob to a walk, which gave the goblins enough time to catch up and start stabbing. Noob saw Greef pull out a mop—the weapon that would claim his life—and scanned the ground for the best place to leave his corpse.

Trumpets blared. Swords flashed around Noob. Bits of dead goblin flew in all directions. When Noob could see again, he saw city guards identical to the ones in the monastery. The goblins had broken their aggro range, and they'd rushed to Noob's aid. And with the goblins dead, they turned their attention to the next threat—the naked dark elf armed with a mop.

Greef tried to flee. The guards caught him just as he'd begun putting his armor back on. They took turns hacking him before Greef gurgled and died, naked but for boots and cape.

A primordial roar carried Reid up from his desk. He punched the air in triumph. "That's *right!* You *like* that? Ride! The! Wave! And! Feel! The! *G's!*" He punctuated each word with a violent pelvic thrust.

He pounced back on his keyboard. "What button was that? What button?"

Noob burst into dance above above Greef's body. "You're dead!" he sang. "You're dead! You're dead, and I'm alive!" and timed each "dead" to a hip-rolling disco thrust. A voice in the back of his head said he should really get inside the city before Greef returned from the dead. Another voice said *fuck that guy.* Noob kept dancing, to the applause of passersby.

A shadow fell over Noob. *Well, it was too good to last.* Noob turned to see what had come to kill him this time.

The man looming over him wore black, riveted armor that looked like it had been made out of a locomotive. His helmet even had a cow catcher in place of a visor. Above the giant's head floated a name: The Truth, Level 100, of <Pwny Xpress>

The Truth was wearing the same knight-flipping-the-bird tabard as Yanker. <Pwny Xpress> must be some sort of team.

The Truth looked from Noob, to Greef's near nude, mop-arm corpse, back to Noob, and applauded.

Noob bowed. The Truth turned to go. "Hey," said Noob.

The Truth turned around.

"Um… if you see Yanker again, could you thank her for helping me out? I kind of got her killed."

The Truth nodded. Noob couldn't tell if that was a yes, or if he was agreeing that her death was his fault.

"Alert!" boomed a voice from the sky. *"Server reset in ten minutes."*

The Truth bowed to Noob, sat, and faded from sight.

Noob peered up at the gates of Marrowstone City. Reid recognized it as the fortress of stone and glass he'd skipped during the opening cinematic. *Shit.* If he'd known he was coming here, he would have paid more attention.

From the center of town, streets branched away from a cobblestone square down cottage-lined roads. Characters of all levels milled around and leapt through the town square, and cryptic chatter flooded the city chat channel:

"LFG Temple of Thunder."

"WTS [Shadowmeld Cloak] 4,000g OBO"

"750 conjurer doin glows outside castle, free with mats"

"Tehr Lehrds ehrf Dehrknehrs now recruiting! Lehrvel 20 Gehrld!"

"WTB runthru Pirates Den 100g"

"rangers are so overpowered"

"shut up fag ur gay"

"CHUCK NORRRISSSS!!!!!"

"Low Low Gold! 10,000g only $39.99! pirates4hire.com!"

"ORLY?"

"YARLY."

Noob wandered, overwhelmed, bumping into every imaginable shade and shape of character. He spotted an elf sitting alone on the steps of the library and jogged over.

"Hey," he started. "Sorry to bug you, but can you help me? I need to find an admin." The elf faded and vanished.

That was rude, he thought. At first. Before he looked around and noticed they were all sitting and fading from sight. *Is the city closing for the night?* "I need to find an Admin! Anyone? An Admin?"

"I'll admin your *doom*, gaywad!"

Trumpets blared. Dueling stones landed around Noob. *"Fyreballz has challenged you to a duel!"*

Noob fled.

Noob darted around a corner and ducked into an alley. Fyreballz dashed past the intersection, flames trailing from his hands. No going back that way.

Noob peered deeper into the alley and noticed a city guard with a bright yellow "A" above his head. He hadn't seen that anywhere else. "Hey, there. Knight guy. Are you an Admin?"

The Knight looked at him. "No, my name is 'A.' Of course I am."

"Didn't know you guys could talk."

"We're not bots, dumbass."

"Alert!" warned the sky. *"Server reset in three minutes!"*

"Make it quick," said the Admin. "Reset in three."

Noob got to it. "I need to find someone. If I give you her name—her real one, I mean—could you give me her info?"

The Admin snorted. "Yes, I am *dying* to get fired. Beat it, stalker."

"Seriously, I know her!"

"Crush on a guildie, huh? Take it from me, she's never gonna go for you, no matter what you do."

"Dude, I'm serious! She's my girlfriend, my fiancée." It was close enough to the truth.

"Jog on, freak. Any other Admin would have reported you by now and banned your ass. Haven't ruled it out myself."

"Fyreballz has challenged you to a duel!"

A ring of dueling stones fell around Noob. "God damn it!"

"It's on, cock-dick!" Fyreballz was blocking the alley, his hands aflame. "Time to flambé the gay away!"

The Admin slowly shook his head at Fyreballz. "This fucking guy. You tormenting noobs again?"

Fyreballs noticed the Admin. The fires around his hands died. "Hey, *he* came on to *me*."

"You know the rules about push-dueling lowbies."

"Come on!" said Fyreballz. "Look at his *name!* He needs fire and *pounding!*"

"He absolutely does. Doesn't matter. This is your second warning. Walk, or it's a one-day ban."

Fyreballz glared at Noob. "You won't always have protection. Roast you later, gayfag." He bounced out of the alley, flinging fireballs at birds.

Blackened pigeons fell around Noob. "Look, man—I hate this game. Most of the things and people I've met have tried to kill me."

"I can see why."

"I don't belong here."

"We are on the same wavelength."

"And I will leave forever the moment I get my girlfriend back. So if you can think of any way you can help me, please —"

"Shut up. The *only* way I'm giving you your girlfriend's info is if you bring me the Godsword."

"Done! Shake on it?"

"There's no macro for that."

"Ah." Noob kicked at the ground awkwardly. "So. Any idea where I find a Godsword? And is it 'God sword' or 'God's word?' They look the same in chat."

The Admin scoffed. "I'm out, bitches." He sat.

"Alert! Server reset in one minute!"

The Admin faded and was gone.

Noob returned to find the town square nearly empty. Only a handful of players remained, and most of them were seated and halfway vanished already.

"Hello?" Nobody was listening. "This may sound like a stupid question, but does anyone know where I can find a Godsword?"

"Alert!" cried the narrator. *"Server reset in five... four..."*

The city began to erase itself. Towers vanished. Houses disappeared. Gray non-space rubbed out the branching side streets one by one.

"Three... two..."

Noob stood alone in what was left of the city: nothing but the cobblestone square, surrounded by gray, formless emptiness.

"One."

A flash of white.

A message popped up on Reid's screen: *Fartherall Online is undergoing routine server maintenance and has gone offline. The adventure continues at 9:00 A.M.* Robo-cowboy tipped his hat with a "Boy, Howdy!" and the game kicked to Reid's desktop.

Reid checked the clock. He blinked a couple of times to see if the numbers would change. They didn't. It really was 4:00 A.M. He'd managed to play through the night.

In a haze, he ambled into the bedroom. *If I go to bed now, I might be able to steal a couple hours' sleep before work. Enough to stumble through the day.* How could he have lost track of time like that?

On the bed was the basket of unfolded laundry, right where Reid had left it. Astrid's camisole was on top. Reid had given it to her on her last birthday, along with the graphics card she'd made extra sure he knew she wanted. It was the camisole she was wearing in the picture of them Reid kept on his desk at work. She hadn't taken it with her.

Reid sat down and started folding the laundry.

4
Making Friends

TIP: If you enjoyed playing with someone, add them to your friends list!

The kitchen on eighth—the one for the non-executives—was a converted office with a microwave, a mini fridge, and no windows. There was a single circular table, but no chairs. The message was clear: if employees wanted to relax, they could do so elsewhere—preferably on their own time.

"I'm surprised you're even vertical," said Lodge.

"Yeah, well." Reid emptied the coffee pot and sugar bowl into his Nalgene bottle.

"You should *not* be in today. There's a reason you have personal days. Isn't she more likely to be playing during the day anyway?"

"I can't afford the time off." He really couldn't, not without Astrid covering her half of the bills.

"Do it anyway," said Lodge. "I'll float you. Forget about the game, about Astrid. You need to take some time for yourself. To adjust."

"I'm getting her back. That starts with getting in touch."

Into the Nalgene went a pint of Half-and-Half. Reid shook it up and chugged half the bottle.

Lodge watched him drink in growing horror. "Dude? You are going to *die*."

The world was a blur. Reid willed it to slow to a normal pace. It did, but the wall of his cubicle wouldn't stop moving. After a second he realized it was because he was bouncing his knee under his desk. He rolled up his grandfather's cuffs and noticed Lodge standing there staring at him.

"Do you want me to get you some water?" Lodge asked. "Or activated charcoal? Maybe a purgative?"

"I'm fine, thanks."

"You look like you ran to work."

"I don't actually recall how I got back to my desk. I may have quantum tunneled."

Lodge started scribbling on paper. "I'm just gonna start filling out the coroner's report now."

"I'm *fine*, ass-hamster. Now let's just assume I remember what we were talking about."

Lodge shrugged, crumpled the page. "So that dude who kept killing you?"

"It's pretty common. People being dicks for the sake of dickdom. I looked it up."

"I've gamed with Cass for fifteen years," said Lodge. "I'm familiar with the concept of griefing. But not everyone was a dick, right? That one player who helped you. Smurf girl. What happened to her?"

Reid shrugged. "I don't know." He left out the part where she might be in hell. "It's too bad. She was the only decent person I met in there."

"You have such a way with women."

Reid stomped on Lodge's foot. Lodge yelped and hobbled off, right through Habermann's aggro range. *Aw, dammit.*

Habermann steamed towards him and steered into his cubicle. "Reid, what does the manual say about horseplay?"

Reid closed his eyes. "Christ, not today."

Habermann kept looking at him. "The manual, Reid."

Reid found the relevant mental file. "Horseplay is not allowed in the office."

Habermann's nostrils twitched. "And personal hygiene?"

"Employees must maintain a clean and professional appearance at all times."

Habermann wiped his brow. "You seem to be forgetting the manual a lot, Reid. That's a shame. That doesn't reflect well on this office."

This is where he'll bring up the Board.

"If they decided to visit today, what would the Board think? The rules in the manual are there for a *reason.* They govern a healthy business. And business is the building block of civilization. Without it, do you know what we have, Reid?"

"Chaos."

"Chaos," said Habermann. "Anarchy. The manual is your bulwark against chaos, Reid. Keep that in mind. You need to be able to demonstrate that you can stick to the rules, that you can set an example."

Reid looked appropriately admonished. Enough so that Habermann nodded—he'd gotten his point across. He set a thick rubber-banded bundle of reports on Reid's desk.

Reid recognized the accounts. They'd taken him three months. "I just finished these."

"You did, and it was well done. But the CEO of

Englebrook-Meyer was indicted this morning, so they suddenly need this year's tax return redone. As well as the last six." Habermann looked over his shoulder towards the elevators. "In here, Sergei."

A janitor wheeled in a furniture dolly full with file boxes. Reid gave it a quick once over, and decided he'd had worse. "That doesn't look so bad."

"Great!" Habermann grinned. "And when you're done with those, the rest are in the conference room."

Reid push-rolled his office chair out of his cubicle. The windowed wall of the conference room was stacked floor to ceiling with file boxes.

Habermann clapped a steak-sized hand onto his shoulder. "Think of this as an opportunity, Reid. To really focus, really *challenge* yourself." Another clap and he was off.

Reid felt a less ample hand on his shoulder and turned to see Lodge.

"What was it Nietzsche used to say?" Lodge asked, with a sympathetic grunt.

"That which does not kill me ruins my life."

Lodge frowned. "I don't think that was it."

"It's what he meant." Reid slumped in his chair and dropped his head. "Any other week, I could handle this."

"Sure, the workload sucks. But look at it this way—you can use this. Focus on it. Plug in some headphones, tune the world out, put the whole Astrid thing out of your mind, and rack up some comp days. There's hours and hours of overtime in there."

"But I've got a lead!" Reid snapped his head back up. "A way to get in touch! I know how to find her!" He leaned conspiratorially towards Lodge, beckoned him into whispering distance.

Lodge leaned forward an inch, and Reid imparted his secret: "The *Godsword*." He infused the word with all proper gravitas.

Lodge nodded back, completely unimpressed. "It's always the hardest right after a break up."

Reid glowered. "We didn't break up."

"Sometimes people go a bit nutty."

"We *didn't break up*."

Reid left the office three hours after everyone else, barely halfway through the first box. He drove home in a zombie state.

From the bedroom, the mattress called to him, singing a siren song of oblivion. *Come to me, lover. Let me take you away from all this. You might even have the dream about pirates.*

"I'll just be an hour," he told his bed.

Noob strode out of Marrowstone City beneath a brilliantly starry sky. He promised the first star he saw that he would make progress tonight. That he would find her. That this would be over soon. The radiant red star—the eye in a constellation of a dragon—seemed to wink back, although that might have just been the frame rate.

A whistle. Noob turned. Greef was standing in front of the gates, between Noob and the entrance to the city. He wasn't alone, either. He'd brought a couple of friends: Fugly the ogre and an orc called Crotch. Each had "Level 100" and <Something Wicked> blazing above their heads.

Greef waved.

Noob looked for the city guards, spotted them staring mindlessly from their posts. Greef and his backup dancers were well out of aggro range. The <Something Wicked> crew drew swords.

Never thought I'd miss Fyreballz. Reid ran.

There was no direction to his flight, no plan. He hugged the road ahead of him as it ran through a village full of players whacking a piñata with a gnome and into the hills beyond, past a sign pointing the way towards Fullvein Mine.

This was enemy territory—computer controlled orcs were patrolling the path ahead. He ran between them. They roared and joined the chase.

Ahead, a cave. Noob plunged through the entrance and darted blindly through twisting tunnels, as orc miners broke away from their work with a roar to chase him.

Noob ran smack into an orc miner—halving his life meter—and fell prone at his feet. The orc howled and raised his pickaxe above his head.

Something stout and wooden hurtled through the air and pinned the orc to the wall. It was the Fullvein Mine sign.

Noob heard a whistle. Greef waved from the mine's entrance, said something in gibberish, and held out his thumb and forefinger an inch apart: "Missed you by *that* much." Fugly and Crotch ran past Greef and killed the angry miners chasing Noob.

More pissed off miners closed in. Noob leapt up and ran around the nearest corner—straight into a dead end.

Before he could turn around, Greef's net pinned him. Noob sighed, accepted his fate, and turned to die.

Greef leapt towards him, blades flashing through the air—and another blade, a huge black one, jumped to block it.

Holding that sword was The Truth—the giant train-faced warrior, the knight on his tabard adamantly giving Greef the finger.

Greef screamed a battle cry, and Crotch and Fugly ran to

flank The Truth. They never reached him. A clutch of arrows from the shadows caught Fugly full in the face, and a fireball exploded against Crotch. And then three figures were on them, swords and staves whirling and striking. Fugly and Crotch shrieked and fell.

The Truth kicked Greef against the wall of the cave. The dark elf sprung to his feet with impossible speed and drove his blade towards the eye slit in The Truth's armor. The bubble of a force field sprung up between them, and Greef's blade skipped off it, sending Greef staggering back.

The Truth swung so hard that his sword sparked as it cut through the air. The blow caught Greef in the neck and golfed his head across the room. It hit the ground a full two seconds after the dark elf's body.

The Truth sheathed his blade and cracked his knuckles.

"Shit." It was all Noob could think to say.

"Well, hey." Yanker stepped into the light of a brazier Noob hadn't noticed. "It's that noob I was telling you about."

"Holy shit," said a voice from the shadows. "His name really *is* Noob. Who does that?"

"If I remember," Yanker said to Noob, "you said I'd never see you again."

Noob wasn't sure what to say. "Sorry to disappoint."

"You even promised."

"To be fair, I *am* a noob," he said. "I suck at stuff. Thanks for helping me not die. Again."

"Well, we did get to kill some nocs, so it wasn't entirely pro bono. And I didn't do it alone. You should thank the rest of the guild."

A tree person stepped out of the shadows. *Dryads—that's what they're called.* She was clad toe to throat in white robes and

61

had flowing Spanish moss for hair, and her name was Bandaid of <Pwny Xpress>. She fake coughed into a barky brown hand—a request for an introduction.

"Really?" Yanker rolled her eyes. "In case you can't read, the super polite one is Bandaid, our healer. She's way into RP."

"You are hurt, young traveler." Bandaid raised a crystalline staff and cast a spell. "Be well!"

A corona of light flared around Noob, and his health bar filled.

"Thy wounds are mended."

"Thank you."

"Thou art welcome."

"Think fast, Noob!" Greef's head flew past Noob's face and stabbed itself into a spike on The Truth's armor. "Aw, come on, Truthy. Don't be a ball hog. Kick it back."

Yanker indicated the speaker. "Our mage."

"Word," said the head kicker, the scantily clad one. "I blow shit up." She was an elf maid named Mansex, also of <Pwny Xpress>. Spider webs would have covered more than the dress she was wearing. She was Level 100, just like the other three.

Yanker pulled Greef's head off of The Truth's armor. "And The Truth is our tank. He stands in front of shit. If you want to make a joke about how he hurts, or will set you free, now's the time."

"We've met, actually," said Noob. "Outside Marrowstone." The Truth nodded by way of greeting.

Mansex spied a patrol of orc miners wandering a nearby passage and casually toasted them with a fireball. "So here's a question," she asked, backlit by miners burning to howling deaths. "How's a Level 1 make it to the back of this mine? This zone's like Level 20, minimum."

"Yes, and however did you escape the clutches of that foul miscreant?"

"The what, now?"

Mansex danced provocatively above Greef's headless corpse.

"Oh. Him. He kept trying to say something to me, but I couldn't understand."

"They scramble in-game chat between factions," said Mansex. "Keeps the death threats to a minimum. You didn't answer the question."

"Oh. No real plan to it," said Noob. "Just ran. French tactics."

"I know not of this 'French,'" said Bandaid.

"You know," said Mansex, "when Chuck Norris runs, he stays in place, and the rest of the world spins like a treadmill."

Noob blinked at her. "What?"

"What is a 'Chuck Norris?'"

"I haven't heard a Chuck Norris joke since 2004," said Noob.

"We have," said Yanker. "Daily."

The Truth just groaned and shook his massive head.

"Oh ye of little faith," started Mansex. "The Church of Chuck shall rise again, oh yes. Even now he watches over us, and one day soon, our savior will return and deliver us with holy roundhouse kicks and sacred beard grooming." The Truth snorted.

"Anyway," Yanker said to Noob, "you still on that bandit leader quest? He's right around here."

"Right here, to be exact." Mansex had abandoned Greef and was now dancing over the corpse of a well dressed orc.

Reid moused over the body. It read *Dromor, Bandit Leader.*

"Um," said Noob, "He's kind of… dead."

"Well yeah," said Yanker. "We kind of killed him."

"A couple hundred times," said Mansex.

Bandaid beamed. "We're searching for hidden treasure, you see."

"Farming a drop," Mansex clarified.

"But he'll respawn soon," said Bandaid. "Return from the dead, I mean."

"And then we'll kill his ass again, along with the rest of him. Unless you'd like a turn."

Dromor's body faded and disappeared. A moment later, he reappeared in a corner of the cave seated on a small stone throne.

"Does anything stay dead in this game?" asked Noob.

"Not really," said Yanker.

"Our world is full of miracles," said Bandaid.

Dromor's eyes locked on Noob, on his Level 1. He snarled "For the Insolace!" and threw himself towards Noob.

A force field bubble surrounded Noob. Dromor's axe bounced off it in a shower of sparks. Noob glanced at Bandaid, who had just cast the spell. The Truth punted Dromor across the room, dropping the orc's health bar to a sliver.

Yanker grinned. "Noob! Finish him off! You remember how."

"I do!" said Noob. He lashed out, whip quick, and touched Dromor.

"That was Pickpocket again," said Yanker.

"Yeah, just realized that," said Noob. "I got a nice knife though."

"Right-click!" yelled Yanker. Reid did.

Noob stabbed Drobor. The orc roared with exaggerated

fervor and dropped dead in the exact same position his corpse had occupied before.

Trumpets blared. An explosion of light rippled up Noob's body, and the number above his head ticked from Level 1 to Level 2 to disembodied applause.

"Huzzah!" cheered Bandaid.

"Ace," said Yanker. "You leveled. Grats."

"I'm so proud," said Mansex, wiping away a fake tear. "Baby's first steps! Now do that 98 more times, you'll be as awesome as us."

"As awesome as *we*," said Bandaid.

Dromor's body began to glow. Noob took a step back. "What's with the corpse? It wasn't doing that last time."

"It means there's treasure," said Yanker.

"Right-click it?"

She nodded.

Reid moved the mouse over the body and clicked. A treasure menu popped up before Noob. In it was the head of Dromor, as well as a second item—a piece of parchment. Noob pulled out the head and examined the bit of paper. "What's a 'Moonchart Fragment'?"

As one, <Pwny Xpress> gaped at him. Then they gaped at each other. The Truth blurted a laugh.

"God damn it." Mansex paced an angry circle around the corpse and punched the wall.

"What karma," said Bandaid. "What cosmic irony."

"God *damn* it!" Mansex cast a spell on Dromor's corpse. The body levitated off the floor. "Rarest goddamn drop, doesn't respawn for *weeks*, and Nooby-Pants here gets it? Eat shriveled leper dick, orc!" She hit the body with a lightning bolt. Burnt orc chunks fountained across the room.

"Fuck," assessed Yanker.

"This is a sign," said Bandaid. "This was not chance! Fortune favors this one, methinks."

"Yeah," said Mansex. "Or he knows *exactly* what he was doing and poached the drop."

Noob wiped Dromor off his face. "It says 'This item begins a quest.' What's that mean?"

"It means you found the drop quest we've been farming," said Yanker. "Try to keep up."

Noob looked up at her. "You were looking for this?"

"For about the last month or so, yeah."

"Hey, it's yours." He offered her the fragment. "I don't need it."

"No dice," said Mansex. "It's bonded to you. It'll be in your inventory until you delete that toon."

"Oh." Noob examined the parchment. It was some sort of astrological chart. One of the constellations looked familiar. "What does it do?"

There was no reply. He looked up to see <Pwny Xpress> circled up and staring at one another. It was eerily quiet but for an occasional shrug or laugh. "Hello? You guys still here?"

"Guild chat," said Yanker. "One sec." They kept conferring. Mansex fireballed another clump of orcs in the hall. Eventually Yanker turned his way.

"So," she said, "we find you amusing. How'd you like to join our guild?"

"For the record," said Mansex, "I voted against you. Because you suck, you see, and I don't have the time to babysit a lowbie."

"I don't know…" said Reid. *This isn't why I'm here.* "I wasn't really—"

"Grab some XP?" continued Yanker. "Finish some quests? Share our loot?"

A bell rang in Reid's head. "Quests! Yes! There's a quest I'm on, actually. I'm looking for the Godsword. Have you seen it?"

Yanker raised an eyebrow. "Funny you should mention that."

"Another sign," said Bandaid.

"Okay, raise your hand if you're *not* looking for the Godsword," said Mansex. "Anyone? No? That's what I thought. I sent that one out over realm chat, by the way. And what's a noob need with the Godsword?"

The guild all looked at Noob for an answer.

"'Tis a fair question, lad."

Noob looked at his feet. "It's kind of embarrassing." That wasn't answer enough for them, so he continued. "I need it to get my fiancée back. I did something I— ... well, I *hurt* her, and she's gone. I don't know where. The Godsword's my only clue. And if I can find that, maybe I can win her back."

Mansex shook her head. "Please tell me that was RP and not IRL."

"Don't be a wanker," said Yanker. "It's real life."

"Oh!" Bandaid's hands fluttered around her face like confused doves. She was so excited she could barely speak. "Oh! Oh, such a noble quest! The search for true love, that which drives us all!"

"Not me," said Mansex. "Beer and pussy, here."

"Silence, whore! Noble Noob," Bandaid took a knee before him.

"Oh, Jesus." Mansex hid her eyes on The Truth's shoulder. He patted her on the back.

"I pledge to thee my aid, my counsel, and my friendship, that you may swiftly find your lady love."

"Thanks," said Noob. What else was he going to say?

Yanker yanked Bandaid back up. "So, what do you say? You'll cover more ground with a group."

Why not? I did promise myself I'∂ make progress tonight. "Sure." Trumpets blared.

A scroll unfurled on Reid's screen: *Yanker has invited you to join Pwny Xpress. Accept?*

Reid clicked "yes."

5
Guild War

*TIP: If you find yourself lost, try asking a
more experienced player for help!*

Yanker escorted Noob out of the mine past row after row of torched orc corpses. The stars were out when they returned to the surface.

Bandaid and The Truth had bid them farewell and logged out in the cave, but Mansex still had a few minutes left on her Empowered Fire buff, and wasn't about to spend that time not setting things on fire. Yanker and Noob could see her in the distance, lobbing balls of glowing death at any hostiles in range.

"You made the right choice," said Yanker. "Guilding up's the way to go. Things are much easier in a group."

"I did make it out of the caves alive," said Noob.

"There you go. It gets harder to solo the higher you go."

"I can imagine."

"Die in pain, man-pig!" An orc leapt at Noob from the cliffside above the cave. Yanker casually stabbed it on the way down.

"Guess she missed one."

Orc miners started to respawn outside the cave, one after

another. Yanker walked right through the middle of them, too high level to pull their aggro. Noob, however, was not.

The nearest orc made it two steps towards Noob before dying on Yanker's sword.

"I wanted to thank you, by the way." Yanker wiped her blade clean. "For coming back for me. After that griefer jumped me in the woods?"

"I thought I'd gotten you killed."

"Well, kind of. I wouldn't have even been in there if I hadn't been running an escort quest for your sorry butt."

"Oh. Sorry."

"*I'll wear your—!*" Skin? Pants? The orc was dead before he could say what.

"But the fact of the matter is," she wiped more blood off her sword, "you came back. Rezzing in that zone, at your level? With a PVP jerk waiting for you? He probably only kept killing you because you kept coming back, and he took it as an insult."

"Ah. So you saw the whole getting-killed-over-and-over thing."

"Some of it. The Truth filled me in on the rest. Nice trick getting the guards to do the dirty work."

"Thanks. Orc."

"I see him." Stab. "Anyway, you coming back like that, dumb as it was—"

"I thought I'd gotten you stuck in Hell."

"Aw, that's so cute! Anyway—" More orcs charged. Her blade whirled. "That was sweet of you."

Three orc heads landed at Noob's feet. "Thanks."

"Ha. You're a good guy, and that's not just the wine talking. Hope your girl appreciates that. So thanks and all."

Noob didn't know what to say. He looked around at the mass of dead orcs arrayed in a near perfect circle around him. "You're welcome. Thanks for adding me to the guild."

"No prob. But you should seriously consider paying the fee to change your name."

"I'm starting to think that. So…" *Focus, Reid. Back on track.* He started down the path back towards the monastery. "The Godsword. When do we go get it?"

Yanker impaled a charging orc and flipped it over her shoulder. "That's an epic quest you're talking about. Not a 'Kill X of Y' or 'Bring me X many troll balls.' That's Level 100 territory."

"But I've got that map," said Noob.

"A *piece* of a map," said Yanker. "The last piece *we* needed."

"Does it show you where the sword is?"

"No," she said, "it shows you where the *door* to the sword is. And the door changes places. It's always at the back of some epic dungeon or another, and it only opens one day a month. For *seven seconds*. And when it closes, it's gone—*poof!*—and appears somewhere completely new one month later. And the only way to find where *that* door is? Is to put together another Moonchart."

Yowza. "But the door goes to the Godsword."

"No, the door goes to the Godsword *dungeon*, which no guild has ever gotten through alive. So unless you've got the map *and* are leveled and geared to the teeth *and* you've got an elite guild to plow your way through the Godsword dungeon, it's not even worth trying."

Noob examined his map fragment. "I'm not finding this encouraging."

"Hey, you're not alone. The Godsword is the single most sought after artifact in the history of, like, ever. They dropped it in the game three years ago and *still* no one's found it, which is *freaking insane* when you think of how much time people put into this game—I mean, you have people *quitting their jobs* to play. *Kids* have *died* from neglect because their parents couldn't pull themselves away, if you can believe that sick shit. People form international guilds to tackle the heavy stuff and quest in *shifts* so there's always someone looking, 24-7. And that's for stuff that respawns! The Godsword doesn't."

"It doesn't?"

"It's an 'it,'" she said, "Singular—as in, there's *one*. It doesn't respawn. You can't come back and kill the same boss for it over and over until you get lucky and the right loot drops. There's only *one* Godsword, across all servers, and once it's found, that's it. Done, finito, thanks for playing. So as you can imagine, there's a bit of competition for it."

Noob nodded slowly. "Okay, so just to confirm: to get my girlfriend's phone number, I have to find the Grail."

She grinned. "That's the long and short of it."

"Could I hire you to find it? You seem really good at stuff."

"I am. But I've got my own plans for it, nooblet. And for *you*—you're part of the team now, you and your delicious bit of Moonchart. Your training begins tomorrow."

Reid was glad his toon couldn't display his nausea. "This is way beyond me."

"Everyone sucks when they start out. But you have to start somewhere. *You* can start by turning in that head. Quests are how you advance. And you're Level 2 now, so you can stealth. I'd like to take a break from orc slicing." She walked towards the road, past orc miners who ignored her.

Noob stood confused for a moment before Reid discovered a new button called "Stealth" on his action bar. He clicked it.

Noob crouched forward slightly and became translucent. He took a step. None of the orcs noticed him. *Well, this certainly would have been useful before.* Noob stealthed his way past the orcs to the road.

When they returned to the chapel, the quest giver had a small treasure box icon floating over his head in place of the scroll.

"Uh..." Noob looked to Yanker for help. "The treasure chest is — ?"

"You've got a completed quest you can turn in to him." Someone screamed in the distance.

"Right. That's what I thought."

"You *can* explore some of this stuff on your own, you know."

"Right-click?"

"Of course." Another scream. Someone was having a bad time outside.

Click.

The quest giver animated. "Well, Noob? Have you brought me the head of Dromar?" When Noob held up the head, the quest giver cheered. "Huzzah! You have proven your worth! Now choose your rewar —"

He screamed and died with a blade sticking out of his face.

Noob blinked. "Did I just...? Was that part of the process?"

A sword tapped Noob on the shoulder. He turned, saw Greef holding it. The dark elf flicked the blood from his blade and sheathed it with a salute.

"You," Noob told him, "are a straight up jerk."

Yanker took a step back. "Back away, Noob."

"I'm tired of this asshole. I've got shit to get done, and not enough time to do it." He stepped up to Greef. "You want to kill me? Fine, go ahead. Hit me, stab me, whack me with your mop. You won't make it past the guards alive." An unpleasant thought occurred to him. "Yanker? Where are the guards?"

Yanker slid her bow off her shoulder. "*Back away,* Noob."

They should be in the narthex. That's where the guard patrols started. Noob looked that way and saw the floor there covered with their dismembered bodies. A small knot of ogres and orcs and lizardmen—<Something Wicked> beneath all their names—surrounded the last guard, who crumpled and died with a whimper.

Greef put two fingers to his mouth and whistled. The Wickeds in the narthex looked up.

"I'm gonna back away now," said Noob.

The Wickeds surged towards the sanctuary.

Yanker fired a glue arrow into the double doors. It stuck them shut. "Stealth!" she yelled at Noob. "Back window!"

The Wickeds smashed through the windows to either side of the doors.

Greef whipped out his net and whirled it over his head. He hesitated a blink when Noob dropped into stealth and vanished—a beat long enough for Yanker to fire a bomb arrow under the altar.

The explosion kicked the big stone slab into the oncoming Wickeds and smashed three of them into hummus.

"Window!" she yelled again.

"I'm sorry," Noob said from nowhere. With his toon translucent, Reid could barely see where he was on screen.

She shot a gray horn-headed Wicked with an arrow that encased him in a block of ice. "Break the damn window!"

Noob looked up. The stained glass window stretched from floor to ceiling and depicted the dragon constellation twinkling.

"That's not vandalism or anything?"

"Oh, my God, how are you so bad at this?"

The quest giver respawned and turned to Noob. "Well, Noob? Have you brought me the head of Dromor?" Greef beheaded him again.

"Window!"

Noob scooped up the quest giver's head and suddenly found himself visible again. *Mental note,* he told himself, *picking up heads turns off stealth.* He chucked the head at the window.

The window exploded in a million rainbow shards. Yanker grabbed him by the collar and leapt out with him before the top panes of the window smashed down behind them, guillotining a pair of Wickeds.

It was chaos outside the monastery. Wickeds were everywhere, ransacking the Human Starting Zone, slaying any questgivers and lowbies they could catch. The chat channel was flooded with realm-wide calls for help. The guards were useless; every time one respawned, a circle of Wickeds smashed it back down.

Yanker read the situation faster than Noob. "This is too well coordinated." She nocked an arrow with a smoking tip to her string. "It's gotta be a full guild raid. Fifty of them at least."

"Fifty?" A dark elf from the nearest squad of Wickeds pointed Noob's way and started casting some sort of fire spell.

"Less talk, more walk." Yanker fired the smoke arrow into the ground. A fog burst up and enveloped them, covering their retreat.

The dark elf wizard finished her spell, and a hail of meteors pounded the earth. When the fog cleared, the ground was dented in hundreds of places and the grass was on fire, but Yanker and Noob were gone.

Hiding in the underbrush at the edge of Inkwood, Yanker and Noob watched the Wickeds burn the Human Starting Zone to the ground.

One knot of raiders had made a game of setting the NPC villagers on fire. Other Wickeds were knocking the heads off merchants. It looked to Reid like they were having some sort of contest to see who could behead which NPC the farthest. It was impossible to tell for sure with the language barrier. But the winner—a hulking ogress named Trinket—did celebrate after she knocked a chandler's head over six houses and a donkey.

"Great distance." Yanker acknowledged. "Did you see the electrical discharge on contact? That's gotta be a Thunderstroke enchantment."

"The village," Noob said. He was hardly attached to the game, but it was still a shock to see his toon's hometown burned to cinders.

"It'll respawn in the morning," said Yanker "The nocs are probably bragging the shit out of this on their channel—look, there's some new ones coming in from other guilds, probably here to see what all the chat was about." Some dueling circles went down between Wickeds and the newcomers. "Shit. They're gonna be here all night."

"We can't get rid of them? Our side, I mean."

"Who's gonna come help? I wouldn't. There's too many of them. And why bother? If our guys are doing anything, they're probably attacking a noc town since so many of their heavies are here."

"Noc?"

"Nations of Chaos."

"If they're noc, then who are we?"

Yanker grinned. "The good guys, obvs."

76

Noob watched the Wickeds cut down a pirate making a desperate break for the edge of town. A small crowd of Wickeds and other newly arrived nocs were following him, taking turns killing him every time he resurfaced.

"What about the lowbies?" Reid asked.

She toed the ground. "Sucks to be them."

"Good guys, huh?" She grinned again.

A ring of dueling stones fell around Noob. *Fyreballz has challenged you to a duel.*

"Oh, a thousand shits!" Reid knew what he'd see before he turned: Fyreballz standing there, hands blazing.

"Aw, yeah!" yelled Fyreballz. "Thought you could escape by getting the town all bizz-urned dizz-own as a distraction, didn't you? Well, *wrong*, gay-bait!" In the dark of the woods, Fyreballz' fire spells lit up like beacons. The Wickeds on the edge of town had to have noticed

Yanker saw Wickeds pointing their way. "Oh, you idiot."

"Should we log out?" Noob asked Yanker.

"Do you want them waiting for you here when you log back in?"

"No. Run?"

"Run."

They plunged deeper into the woods.

Fyreballz whistled. The amplified pitch got the attention of everyone in town and a few folks half a zone over. Fyreballz threw a fireball high up into the woods, where it shone like a magnesium flare, lighting up everything below.

Greef shrieked an order, and the Wickeds hurtled into the woods.

Fyreballz cast an illusion on himself and disappeared. "That's what you get for not dueling me, homofag!"

Noob surged through the woods after Yanker. "Stay on the path stay on the path stay on the path—"

"Shut up! Here!" She pulled him off the path and dragged him right past a cluster of goblins. They giggled and skipped merrily after him.

So this is how I die, thought Noob. "Where are we going?"

"Wwere gonnsa hold up tikl they stopp chasing ud." Was Yanker's reply.

"What?"

"Sry typing with onew hamd."

She led him deeper into the woods. They bounced down mossy moguls and scattered a flock of Level 50 dire crows. The wooden fortress-complex they'd passed the night before loomed ahead of them. Its entrance was circular, but the circle was full of a strange oily blackness.

"Throu ther1!"

Noob ground to a stop. The circle in the door was black as pitch and had an odd depth to it. Iridescent shimmers danced over its surface. "What the hell's in the door?"

Yanker abruptly hugged him. A rain of arrows slammed down around them. Several hit Yanker with wet, meaty smacks. Her health bar dropped to a third. "Go in, or we're dead!" she said. "And don't *move* in there, or you're dead."

Noob blinked. "Are you *sure* this is the best—?"

She kicked him through the circle.

A loading screen for the Moonhollow Dungeon filled Reid's monitor. The graphic behind the status bar depicted an open-roofed wooden castle. Robed cultists worshipped a hideous, horned thing with rows of shark-like teeth.

Reid watched the loading bar fill.

Noob shot out the other side of the black circle and landed on his face. He rolled over and examined the portal: he could see Inkwood beyond, but the colors were inverted, like a film negative. He couldn't see Yanker, or the goblins, or the Wickeds.

With a weird *crack-splash*, the circle spat Yanker at him. She tucked, flipped, and alighted on her feet. She glanced down at Noob, still spread-eagled on the floor. "It's okay. It can take years to stick the landing."

She helped Noob up. Ahead, the wooden walls opened into a grove littered with fallen monoliths, their stone weathered and overgrown with moss.

"Don't. Move." said Yanker. "They notice us, we die. And by 'we,' I mean 'you.'" She indicated knots of cultists—*the robe guys from the loading screen*—meditating in appropriately spaced clusters throughout the complex. "The lower your level, the more you aggro. In here, you're a big shiny appetizer with a siren."

Noob glanced back at the portal. "Something Wicked—"

"Can't follow us. That black circle? That designates an instance. When you go through, you and whoever you're grouped with get their own version of the dungeon, their own *instance* of it. Keeps guilds from swarming the place."

"So they can't come through?"

"If they do, they'll be in their *own*, parallel version of the dungeon. Make sense?"

"Still no."

"Eh, don't lose sleep over it. We'll just hang here until it's safe to go back out."

"Can I log out now?"

"Not in an instance. Sorry."

"Is there another way out?"

"At the very end, after the end boss."

"Oh. Would you mind killing us a path?"

"This is a level cap dungeon," she said. "I can't solo in here."

Noob peered at the cultists. Their levels ranged from 99 to 102. *Ouch.* "So our options are…?"

"I told you. Wait them out." Yanker stretched, sighed. "So. Wanna tell me why those guys have such a hate-on for you? Now that you've dragged us into some kind of crazy guild war?"

Noob shook his head. "I really don't know. I got Greef killed once, outside Marrowstone. Twice, if you count when you guys got him in the cave."

"Uh huh. And how many times did he kill you?"

"Uh," Reid thought back. "Three times. In the woods. No, two—it was the goblins the first time. So yeah, twice."

Yanker grinned. She burst out laughing. "That's it! Oh, my God, that's brilliant! You're *tied*!"

"It wasn't even me who killed him."

"Doesn't matter! That's the beauty of it! This is a PVP server. He had engaged you in combat—you, a Level 1!—both times he got dropped! You know what that means? You're *tagged* in those kills! Do you have *any idea* what that's done to his PVP rating? He's tied with a *Level 2* for head-to-head kills. Oh, that's rich. I've half a mind to roll a NOC alt just so I can give him shit." She laughed again. When he didn't respond, she smacked him in the chest. "Come on, it's funny."

Reid allowed Noob a chuckle. "Okay, yeah, it is."

"Damn right it is."

A patrol of cultists was heading their way. Noob dropped into stealth.

"Good call," said Yanker. "Still, to be safe, I'm gonna distract them." She drew a flare arrow out of her quiver, pulled it to her ear, and the Wickeds came through the instance.

On instinct, Yanker whirled and fired her flare arrow right into Greef's eyes. The flash blinded everyone and whited out Reid's screen.

When it faded, Noob found Yanker dragging him by the back of his shirt down the corridor past dazed and blinded cultists. She threw him behind a fallen monolith and dove down beside him.

"Bull*shit*," she spat. "How the *hell* did they get in *our* instance?"

"I thought you said they couldn't—?"

"They *can't*!"

"Then what are they doing here?"

"Duh, looking for us. Keep your head down."

The Wickeds—Reid could see five of them—got their sight back about the same time as the cultist patrol. With no other targets visible, the cultists attacked the Wickeds. The Wickeds fell upon them in a flurry of blades and magic.

The first cultist dropped. "They're winning," said Noob.

"Let me see if any other guildies are on," said Yanker. She fell silent for a second. "Just Mansex. Better than nothing, I guess."

"I thought she logged out."

"She's leveling one of her alts, a paladin called Cockstorm. Can't believe they haven't made her change that. She's switching over now."

"Sup, bitches," typed Mansex over guild chat. "Oh, a Moonhollow run? Sweet, I'll teleport right there."

"Um," said Noob. "You should probably—" Yanker hushed him.

81

Mansex materialized in an explosion of light, just as the final cultist fell. The Wickeds locked eyes on her. "What the f—?" was all she managed before the first arrows hit her.

"Now!" said Yanker. "Run for the instance!" She led the way past the distracted Wickeds, back towards the entrance. Mansex screamed and died.

"You blue-assed bullfucker!" typed Mansex. Apparently, even if you were dead, you could talk to your friends. *Mediums must have it hard here.* "I can't *believe* you used me as bait! Not cool!"

"Sorry," said Yanker. "I'll give you an extra share on the next run, promise." She turned a corner—and skidded to a halt as another five Wickeds shot in through the instance. "Oh, suckpuppies." She dove behind a tree.

The new Wickeds ran past Yanker's hiding spot to join their guildmates, who had already engaged the next cluster of cultists. "How are they doing this?" said Yanker.

"You know," said Mansex. "I heard rumors there's this mod you can download. Fourth Wall Break, I think it's called. It's supposed to let you follow someone through an instance."

"That's *so* illegal!"

"Yeah. Want to report them?"

"Um," said Yanker. "Where's our Noob?"

"Noob?" said Mansex. "You brought *Noob*? He's absolute meat in here! I approve, you're forgiven."

Noob had fled when the new squad of Wickeds arrived, and stealth-run blindly back through the dungeon. Cultists passed him running the other way to attack the Wickeds, and they either couldn't see through his stealth or didn't bother with the lowbie in the corner when there were level capped players to kill.

Noob had wound up in what he assumed was the end boss's chamber, based on the hulking shark-toothed elk-thing pacing in a circle of cultists. Noob had stealthed gingerly around the rim of the room and discovered a door behind the boss. Through the peephole in the door, he could see another shimmering black circle.

"I found the exit," he chatted to his group. "Door's right here. Behind some sharky elk guy."

"Wendigo," corrected Mansex.

"I'll meet you outside."

"No, don't!" yelled Yanker. "*Stop!*"

Noob opened the door and suddenly unstealthed.

"When you touch something," explained Yanker, "you break stealth."

Noob looked over his shoulder. The Wendigo was licking its lips. "I really, really wish I'd known that." The Wendigo unleashed a bloodcurdling scream.

The Wendigo's footsteps shook the corridor behind Noob as he ran back the way he came. When it got within striking range, it roared and grabbed for him.

A force bubble sprung up around Noob. The Wendigo's claws bounced off and sent Noob (bubble and all) bouncing like a superball down the hallway—right past Bandaid.

"Huzzah!" cried Bandaid. "I got you! Sorry I couldn't arrive sooner."

The bubble-shield bounced into a circular grotto, landed in the middle of the Wickeds, and popped.

Greef grinned down at him and said something in gibberish. The Wickeds laughed.

Noob smiled. "If you like me, you'll love my new friend."

The Wendigo burst into the room with a roar—all claws

and antlers and slathering maw—and waded into the Wickeds. It kicked Fugly through a stalagmite and bit Crotch clean in half. The remaining Wickeds scrambled to escape the monster.

Noob crawled away, and Bandaid helped him to his feet. "Noble Noob. Couldst thou please explain what's going on?"

"I really can't."

Yanker ran up, pointed at Mansex's abandoned body. "There!"

Bandaid spotted her body. "Oh, cruel fates! Our friend has fallen, alas!" She burst into tears.

"Stow the RP." Yanker eyed the Wickeds. "They're working their way through the Wendigo." Even with the drop it had gotten on them, the Wickeds had knocked out half its hit points already.

Bandaid stood above Mansex and started casting. "Today, we right a grave injustice! Today, we snatch our friend back from the hands of Death!"

"Heh," typed Mansex. "You said snatch."

"Come back to us!" pled Bandaid. "The book of your life has chapters yet unwritten!"

Noob fell in beside Yanker. "Is she always like this?"

"Yep."

The Wendigo fell to a quarter of its life. A dead Wicked dropped from its antlers.

"By the Light and the Gods Above, I command you to live! Live *again!*" A pillar of holy light erupted under Mansex and carried her to her feet. Bandaid collapsed dramatically. "It is done."

"Right," said Mansex. "Let's do this shi—"

A net landed over Mansex and Yanker. Bandaid popped to her feet.

Greef had spotted <Pwny Xpress> and torn himself away from the Wendigo battle. He rapped Bandaid behind the ear with a sap, flattening her again. The Wendigo dropped the second to last living Wicked.

Greef drew his sword. Noob drew back. With a scrambled curse, Greef slashed Noob across the face, dropping his hit points to single digits.

The Truth barreled past Noob and caught Greef's next blow on his shield. He bashed Greef backwards a good ten yards.

Greef howled in frustration as the Wendigo bit his head off. With the final Wicked in the place dead, the Wendigo fixed its attention back on its original target: Noob.

The Truth cut Yanker and Mansex free. "Fall in!" yelled Yanker. She nodded to The Truth. "Glad you could make it, by the way." The Truth nodded.

The Wendigo charged Noob. The Truth planted himself before the Wendigo and hacked at it with its every step. Mansex slowed its pace by half with an ice bolt while Bandaid cast a spell over them all, and their health bars spooled up. Yanker pumped the Wendigo full of arrows—poison arrows, barbed arrows, arrows that exploded on impact and at least one that erupted in a shower of fireworks until its life meter was so low he could hardly see it.

"Noob!" she yelled. "Finish it off! *No dancing this time!*"

Noob drew his knife and hurled it at the Wendigo.

The Wendigo bellowed, arched, and fell dead with Noob's knife in its knee. Noob leveled six times in machine-gun bursts of light.

A sudden quiet descended. The guild circled up, looked around. Everything else in the room was dead: the cultists, the Wickeds, the Wendigo. Total carnage.

"Can we dance now?" asked Noob.

The Truth nodded gravely as the rest of <Pwny Xpress> burst into dance.

"Hells, yeah!" shouted Mansex. "Pwned and disowned!" Her clothes vanished down to her skivvies. She shook her wares in the Wendigo's face. "Chuck Norris could have done it better, but only by a factor of several thousand."

"And now," said Bandaid, "if nobody minds, I shall resume my studies."

"Not a problem," said Yanker. "Thanks for saving our bacon."

"We should all jet," said Mansex. "It's about a two minute run from the nearest Underworld entrance. The Wickeds have probably rezzed there by now."

"Right," said Yanker. "Everyone out."

"Just one sec," said Noob. "There's something I gotta do." He knelt down by Greef's body and whispered: "Three to two."

He rose to find Yanker grinning at him. "Hey," she said, "you wanna see a dragon?"

6
Painkiller Dreams

*TIP: Healing potions can be purchased from most vendors.
If you have the right skills, you can make your own!*

Yanker led Noob to a corner of the Inkwood where a meadow was hidden behind the crest of a thorn-crowned hill. Reid followed her instructions this time and they arrived without incident. Below them, a line of flowering trees ringed an idyllic glade. A colossal dragon paced around the glade, moonlight glittering off blood-red scales.

"Pretty cool, yeah?" Yanker asked from over his shoulder.

"Yeah," said Noob. "Wow." He didn't really have anything to compare it to. It was larger than any animated thing he'd seen in the game. He also didn't see any other animal life here, and no monsters aside from the dragon. "So... why's it here? What's it do?"

"That's just it," she said. "Nothing. There's no reason for it to be here. None."

Noob blinked at her. "I don't follow."

"It's not guarding a dungeon. It doesn't drop any treasure. It's just *here*, this big awesome beautiful dragon that'll tear your damn head off if you pull aggro. Maybe they'll put an instance here in an expansion or something. That's kind of the theory at the moment. But for right now, it's just this insanely powerful dragon in this pretty little valley." She sat down on the grass, put her bow to one side, and stretched.

The dragon completed its circuit and began another. "So... wait. There's got to be more to it than that. This isn't part of a quest or anything?"

"Nope."

"What level is it?"

"High." She grinned. "It doesn't have one. It also doesn't give experience, so groups can't just come in here and mine it for XP. No loot, no achievement, nothing. It *is* super powerful, though. Like end-boss tough."

"Then why's it here? What's the point?"

"There isn't one."

"There *has* to be. A game like this... I mean—okay," he pointed at the dragon, "we've gotta be looking at hundreds of hours of design and animation. No company's going to invest resources like that without a way to monetize it, but you're saying they just put it out here to pasture?"

"What does it matter? It's just nice. I thought you'd like it."

"I'm lost."

She flung her arms out. "Oh, my God, it's quiet! It's pretty! It's a nice place to be!"

Noob looked over his shoulder, out the ring of trees. "The Wickeds won't find us here?"

"Nobody comes here. I've spent hours here without seeing another player." She patted the ground next to her. "Come on. Sit."

Noob sat. There *was* something oddly peaceful, almost

hypnotic about watching the behemoth lumber around the little garden. "It is nice, I guess," he admitted. "Reminds me a little of Point Defiance. The trees, I mean. Not the dragon."

"Isn't it just the most beautiful thing you've ever seen?"

"No." Reid grinned. "It's cool, but not even close."

"Okay, then what is? No, I got it—your girlfriend. 'She's the most adorable thing ever beheld and we shall have gorgeous and well behaved babies.'"

"Closer. Still no. Don't tell her I said she wasn't, though."

She turned to him. "Well then what is? Now I *am* curious."

"My grandmother's hair." She blinked at him. "She always had the one same hairstyle. The only one I could remember, at least. It was this bun thing, always just, you know, *perfectly* in place. And she always wore it that way. Even in pictures... same hair, even when she was my age. Jet black; I always figured she dyed it. Anyway, a week before she died—she was pretty much already gone from the dementia by this point—we're moving her into hospice care, and my aunt brings her out after a bath, and she's in her pajamas, and her hair's just... different. Because up till that moment, I'd never known she was wearing a wig.

"Instead of the bun, her hair is this beautiful wavy white. Like snow on a riverbank. And it's hanging to her shoulders, and it was singly the most beautiful and saddest thing I'd ever seen. Because she wasn't *there*, you know? I mean, she *was*, but... shit. You know about dementia?"

"Yeah. It hit my Gramps."

"And I told her she was beautiful, and she smiled at me, and had no idea who I was. It was the most... like, it was the first time I'd ever *really* seen her, you know? And I'm like, why would you *hide* this? This beauty? Why keep this part of you a secret? I'm sure my Grandpa knew. Why put forward a lesser version of yourself?"

They sat in silence for a bit. The dragon completed another loop.

"So anyway," said Noob, "that's the prettiest thing I've seen."

"Wow. Well, *I* sure feel shallow."

"I don't know why I told you that," said Reid. "Sorry if it was weird."

"It's because we're anonymous. Same reason people go to therapists. It's safe to unload to someone who'll never be part of your outside life."

"I guess that's true." Reid had never told Astrid. He assumed she wouldn't want to know because she needled him so much about his grandfather's wardrobe. Now he wished he had.

Yanker sighed, stretched out on her back. "This valley… it's perfect. After a long day of grinding, I can just sit here for hours, just to be, relax."

"Really? For hours?"

"Mm hm."

"You sound like Astrid. But why play the game if you're not going to, you know, play?"

Yanker propped herself up on her elbows. "I don't *play* here, Noob. I live here. This is the only world I give a fuck about." She smiled.

Or rather, her avatar smiled. Reid was looking at an animated model of a projection of someone else; not a person. He knew that intellectually, but in that moment, it was hard not to take what she said at face value.

"I really don't get you," he said, finally.

Yanker chuckled and lay back down.

Noob heard a mechanical buzzing in the distance and wondered if that meant the Wickeds had tracked them down. "Do you hear that?"

"Hear what?"

The buzzing wasn't coming from the computer, Reid realized after a moment. He peeled himself away from the screen and ambled his way to the bedroom. His alarm clock was blaring. 6:00, the day was calling.

Reid wished for the life of him that he could stay home. Not to sleep—though he desperately needed that—but to stay in the clearing with the dragon. With Yanker.

In the office kitchen, Reid watched the last of the coffee trickle down into the pot. When it had stopped dripping, he poured the pot back into the coffee maker and started a new batch. Coffee filtered through coffee. It came out looking like used motor oil.

"What the hell is that?" Lodge had followed the smell of burning grounds to the kitchen and found Reid standing there dead-eyed. "No sleep again?"

"I don't know. I'm not entirely convinced I'm not dreaming this."

Lodge waited until the last co-worker had left and shut the door behind him. "Listen, Tit-Whistle... Why don't you come stay with me for a little while? I'm worried about you."

"I'm fine, Nipple-Dick," croaked Reid.

"You're making coffee squared."

"Cubed. I already had a pot in the reservoir before this one."

"This is not healthy behavior. I'm afraid to leave you alone."

"I'm not alone." Reid smirked. "I've got a *guild*. We've got matching tabards and *everything*." He pulled out the pot and poured the caffeinated sludge into his Nalgene.

"Is there anything I can say that will get you to take a day off—a *real* one, not one spent at your computer? And maybe also pour that poison down the sink?"

Reid swirled sugar into the slurry. "Why couldn't I have just been happy? I didn't have anything to complain about. Not really. She's out of my league, you know. Always has been."

"Dude."

"It's just a phase. I could have just ridden it out. Cutting that cord? That's not me."

"Dude. She bailed on your anniversary. Your *anniversary*."

"Personal anniversary." He took a sip from the pot. "Not like it was anything official."

"It's been—what, a week now?" Lodge asked. "The whole waiting in the game for her to discover you thing? It was cute. Probably seemed romantic at the time, I don't know. Like running to the airport to catch her before she gets on the last flight to Paris."

"What?"

"Point is, it's not cute anymore. The cute waveform has collapsed. Now it's just sad and creepy."

Reid stopped stirring. "There's blame on both sides here."

"I don't get it," said Lodge. "I really don't get it. No sex in the world could be good enough. Why you've put up with her as long as you have, I just—I mean, if it were *me*—"

"Because she's all I *get!*" Reid slammed his hand down and heard a smash. There was hot pain in his hand and leg. He looked down to see shards of coffee pot on the counter and floor. A puddle of coffee was spreading at his feet, and there was glass shrapnel in his wrist. It didn't hurt as much as the pain in his chest.

"She was the only girl who ever looked at me," he said to Lodge. "Pretty has nothing to do with it. I wouldn't have cared what she looked like. She *picked* me." The pain in his wrist was a dull ache. Distant, curious—a minor nuisance. "I'm not good at alone."

"Yeah," said Lodge. He took the handle of the broken coffee pot out of Reid's hand, led him to the sink, and ran warm water over his wrist while he picked out bits of glass.

"It was fate," Reid was saying. "That's the only thing it could have been. That dumbass ASB rally."

Lodge pressed a wad of paper towels against his wrist.

"That wasn't just chance. It couldn't have been. I've never shown any athletic ability before or since. It was meant to be." He didn't flinch when Lodge applied a disinfectant from the kitchen first aid kit. "And who were we then. Kids? I've known her longer than I've been out of puberty. She's been there, she's been here, for everything."

Lodge wrapped a bandage around the worst of it. Blood was already seeping through. "You need to see a doctor."

Reid nodded. "She was always there. When we walked into that cheese shop on spring break. In Oregon, at Fort Stevens, when we got biblical in the shipwreck—God *damn*, that was cold. She was there when my sister got married. We were both in the wedding party. We escorted each other down the aisle during the procession. I told her 'We should give this a try sometime, just the two of us.' She punched me."

"I'm taking you to the hospital."

Reid watched Lodge lead him towards the door and say something to a wide-eyed intern.

"She was there when my nephews were born. Every Thanksgiving. When my grandparents died." Reid's face scrunched up. "I don't know me without her." Tears squeezed out of his eyes. "I miss my Grandpa."

"I know you do, man. He was a great guy. Awesome fashion sense."

"I'm very, very tired."

"I'll bet you are." The intern returned with Lodge's keys.

"What happened to my arm?"

"Bunch of ninjas. Came out of nowhere."

"Did we beat them?"

"Yeah. You kicked six out a window. I'm taking you to the hospital because you overdosed on awesome."

"Sweet. Can we stop for coffee?"

"Absolutely not."

The last time Reid had been to Tacoma General was the last time he'd seen his grandfather.

His grandmother had passed six months earlier. Grandpa Frank had been blindsided by an Alzheimer's diagnosis around the time Reid started college, and had kept it hidden from the family for years, until his wife's illness made that impossible. At her funeral, he had a moment of clarity when he saw his wife lying in her casket. Frank had leaned over her, kissed her forehead, and told her he'd see her soon.

Frank had been pretty much out of it the last time Reid had visited him in the hospital. The family had been coming in from across the country to pay their respects. It had been obvious that Frank didn't recognize most of them, but he'd always put on a smile and made small talk to cover up for it.

Every hour or so that Reid spent at his bedside, Grandpa

would notice him and his face would light up. "Frankie!" he'd yell, and grab Reid's hands. Even in his 80s, the retired aluminum worker had a grip like iron.

"I'm Reid, Grandpa," he'd say. "Frankie's boy."

"Oh. Is he working, or getting something to drink?"

"He's working." Reid's dad hadn't visited.

"Well, when he comes, send him my way. I'm gonna get him straightened out."

After the third day, Reid had stopped correcting his grandfather and started answering as his dad. He heard the same stories over and over. Growing up in Tacoma when it was the big city in the state. His favorite World War II joke. Taking that beautiful Korean girl to the dance on base, and not being able to speak a single word to her not because of the language barrier, but because he was so damn nervous.

And Reid, in turn, told Grandpa what he wanted to hear from his son. He was working again, a good union job. He'd gotten back together with Cathy. Little Reid would be a big brother soon. He could see the tears swimming in his grandfather's eyes. His son had gotten things straightened out. He didn't need to know that Frank Jr. was sharing a house in Idaho with three other divorcés whose favorite pastime was drinking and dwelling on how badly life had screwed them.

Reid had saved his tears until the rest of the family had gone home and Frank had slipped asleep. He would stay strong for his grandfather, for his grandparents. Making Frank's transition easier for him was the least he could do.

Reid hadn't learned until he was applying for college that his grandparents had legally adopted him when he was seven. He remembered going to live with them, of course. The weekends when his dad left him with his grandparents had become weeks, and then months, and eventually the little house in Tacoma had become his permanent address. Frank Jr. always swore he was coming back, and that he'd be coming back with everything he'd slowly lost to the bottle. Reid remembered standing at the window, watching his father drive away after one of his increasingly infrequent visits.

"You can always grow into your life," Grandma Seunghye had told him. It was like her favorite chapter from the Tao Te Ching. *The greatest good is like water. It brings life to the Ten Thousand Things and does not strive. It flows in places men reject and so is like the Tao.* If anyone had known about going with the flow, it was Grandma. She'd left Seoul at eighteen, a war bride to an American GI, heading to a country she didn't know with a man she'd only just met. What right did Reid have to complain?

And so Reid had grown up with grandparents for parents, and theirs was the life he had grown into. He wore slacks instead of jeans, usually a vest or tie. He actually enjoyed Lawrence Welk. He mastered pitch and dominoes and was routinely beating Frank at cribbage in the years before the Alzheimer's. If he hardly fit in at school, it didn't much bother him. He had the people who mattered most in his corner. And when they died, everything had fallen apart.

The night Frank died, Reid had fallen asleep at his bedside. He had woken up to an iron squeeze on his arm.

"Reid," Frank had said to him, his eyes remarkably clear. "I have to go now."

Reid had swallowed his tears and nodded. There was no point fighting it. "Okay."

"You've got a good woman there, Frankie. You hold on to her." He was seeing Reid's father again.

"I promise." He would never disappoint Grandpa, not if he

could help it.

"Good." Frank gave his arm another good squeeze. "Hey." He elbowed his grandson, a twinkle in his eye. "I ever tell you the one about the Norwegian fighter pilot?"

Only a thousand times. I would hear it a thousand more. "No, Grandpa. Please tell me."

Reid watched the bowl turn circles in the microwave. He wasn't hungry, but he was supposed to take the pain meds with food. The stitches in his wrist itched, like wearing a shoe with the laces too tight—he wanted to dig in there with his fingers, or maybe a drain snake, and just *scratch.*

The microwave beeped. He took the bowl of french onion soup out with an oven mitt and dropped a fat slab of gruyere on top.

A message from Yanker was waiting for him when he got back to the computer. *We'll start with the Marrowstone Underground quest chain. It's a long one, but you'll level a bunch.*

Noob propped the soup on his desk and typed back: *How long? Do I have to finish the whole thing?*

Reid could almost hear her sigh through the monitor. *To qualify for the Godsword quest, you have to be at the level cap. That means you need to go up 92 levels in two weeks, which equals twelve to fifteen hours of play per day, EVERY day. So YES, you have to finish the whole quest chain.*

Reid grimaced. He eyed the stack of bloodstained file folders he'd snatched as Lodge was marching him out of the office. *Not like I have anything else going on*, he typed back.

Keep that pace, you'll hit 100 right in time for the Moonchart door to open.

Swell, he typed. The itching was driving him crazy. He held his arm over the soup. The steam coming off it felt good, but made the urge to scratch that much worse. He put a towel over his wrist and scratched that instead.

You there? He'd been quiet for about a minute.

Not like I have a choice, he wrote back, *but yeah.*

What's eating you?

Not a big fan of life right now. He'd scratched too hard and his wrist was bleeding again. He rewrapped the towel around it, lifted the bowl, blew on a spoonful.

Well, just remember, Yanker chatted at him. *That which does not kill you ruins your life.*

Reid dropped the soup in his lap.

Yanker was seated under a beach umbrella in the dragon's glen and looking at him quizzically. "You okay?"

"Soup in my lap," said Noob. "My grandchildren are screaming."

"Do you need help? IRL?"

"No, the soup's cooling off and the meds just kicked in. Now I'm just damp and kind of warm."

"I'm gonna go ahead and change the subject, if you don't mind."

"Please."

"So. After the Underground chain, there are a number of routes we can take to get you to the cap. I'll pull the guild together, and we'll power level you the rest of the way. The only question then will be what we're going to do with the Godsword when we find it."

"I'm gonna get things back to the way they were," Noob said. "The way they're supposed to be. And after that, I'm going to stop playing this colossal time suck."

"Aw, I bet you'd stay. You could play as a couple. How much fun would that be?"

"I have no idea."

"Are you gonna tell me how the two of you met up?"

"Really? You want to know that?"

"Mainly I want you to stop bitching. But yeah, sure."

"I made a half-court shot."

"No shit? You win the big game or something?"

"Not really. Our student government—this was back in high school—they used to have a raffle at halftime during every basketball game. If they pulled your name, you got the chance to win a few 24-packs of soda."

"But you had to sink a half-court shot to win."

"Right. And so nobody'd ever made it, and the prize kept getting bigger. 'Cause they kept adding more packs each time. It became kind of a joke. The stack got so big they had to wheel it out on a cart."

"And they drew your name."

"Yeah." He hadn't even planned to be there, but his grandparents insisted he go do something social instead of spending another evening at home with them. He had checked the school calendar and attended his one and only high school basketball game.

When they'd drawn his name out of the fishbowl and called it out, jeers and laughs had rained down. The weirdo kid in the suit was going to take the shot? Hilarious!

Reid had tried to slink away, but the cheerleaders spotted him and dragged him to midcourt. Camera phones flashed all around him. The Associated Student Body president smirked and slapped the ball into his hands.

Reid didn't even want to be there, and he wasn't going to

99

make the shot anyway. So if he was going to miss, he was going to do it in style. He turned his back to the basket, put on his sunglasses, and hurled the ball over his shoulder. Nothing but net.

The place exploded. Reid had never been cheered before. The benches emptied. A tsunami of screaming students slammed into him and carried him (and his soda) out of the auditorium on their shoulders—smashing his head against the top of the doorframe in the process.

When the stars faded, Reid saw the popular black-haired cheerleader who'd stopped to help him up. That was how he'd met Astrid. "We've been together ever since."

"Wow," said Yanker. "Shit. With a meet like that, you have to be destined for each other. It's like a fucking John Hughes movie."

"Yeah." Reid left out the part where Astrid had dragged him to the party afterward. The atmosphere was nothing he'd experienced before, all noise and smoke and bodies wriggling against each other. No Lawrence Welk music here. Suddenly he was Mr. Popular—doubly so because he had donated the mixers (his soda). Astrid never left his side, and spent the party wearing his blazer and introducing him around and laughing at the goose egg on his forehead. And near the end of the party, with only stragglers still conscious, she had taken his virginity under the piano.

Reid had come so hard he had cracked his head on the undercarriage and swore a symphony. He could still feel that amazing mix of bursting pain and brilliant bliss.

Astrid had laughed. "I like you," she said. "I'm gonna keep you." And in that moment he fell.

Yanker broke his reverie. "You still there?"

"Yeah." Reid tried to recall what they'd been talking about. *Right. That stupid Grail sword.* "So, the Godsword. What would you do with it?"

"Wave it around," she said, "every chance I get. And then put it on my resume. Talk about a branding masterstroke, right? That would get Boy Howdy's attention. Maybe then I could get hired and tell them everything they need to fix about their game."

"I thought you... fix? Meaning there's something wrong? You love this game."

"I do," she said. "It's the realest world I know. But it's changing. They're losing players to the new consoles and mobile, which, you know, is gonna *happen.* Trends change. But this game's been around a decade because it offers something those *can't*—these totally immersive, massive and heavily populated areas that feel... organic. *Real.* Right? *Like you're not playing a game.*"

"But it is a game."

"No, it *looks* like a game. What it is, is a *world*. It lets you make mistakes. It lets you explore the edges. You can go to the 'Here Be Dragons' part of the map if you want, and you'll get your arse handed to you, but you have the *option*. The game's not on rails. It's not prompting and poking you to try this next, learn this obvious mechanic, download this new content, come back in six hours or pay us a dollar to get the next quest *now*. All that shit just reminds you you're playing a game, and that games are business, and that you're a fucking customer. Breaks the immersion. It takes you out of the game.

"That's not why I'm here," she continued, "and I *hate* that we're starting to see that crap. The too-easy starting zones, letting new players *begin* with toons at the level cap... letting you specialize in *all* your class's talents — for a fee, of course — instead of having to make a decision and, you know, build relationships and tactics and *learn how to survive.* Stop making the content *consumable,* stuff you buy instead of *doing.* If everyone can do it, it stops being special. Like that," she said, pointing at the dragon.

"I get it," said Noob. "You're like a virtual environmentalist."

"Ha! I like that. I'm gonna use that in conversation."

Noob regarded her levelly. "What kind of work would you want to do there?" he asked. "That was a pretty intuitive analysis."

"Design." Her eyes lit up. "Game design."

"No shit."

"Yeah. I've shipped a couple games on my own, but I could never get hired anywhere."

"Why's that?"

"Hi, I'm a woman." The ground rumbled as the dragon tromped by.

"Well, if you've made games, isn't that kinda the criteria?"

"Should be. Mine were little ones, Kickstarter games. Stuff I could solo on the coding side and just outsource the art from campaign funds."

That's incredible. "Anything I would have played?"

"Probably not."

"What were they called? So I can look them up?"

"Please don't. I made the mistake of appearing in the pitch video. First time I'd done that. The comments... fuck. Even fucking industry blogs, it was all how fuckable I wasn't. And how obviously my boyfriend was the designer, or how I must have totally ripped off this game that launched two weeks *after* my campaign because I was a fucking stupid slut who could *never* have designed anything like that myself.

"So, yeah. Not going down that road again. I'm done. Got out before it could suck the joy out of playing. The Godsword—it's a hell of a trump card, you know? 'I got the thing you *couldn't*, fuckers, so I'm a *better* gamer than you and *suck on that!*' Maybe with something like that under my belt, it'd be easier to walk past the other shit if I ever went back, you know?"

"Shit," said Noob. "I really hope you find the sword." *It's a shame we couldn't both.* There was only the one Godsword, she'd told him, and once that's found, that's it. *Done, finito, thanks for playing.*

Yanker grinned. She pulled a baguette out of her picnic basket and took a bite. "Mmm. Tastes like mac and cheese. My dinner," she explained.

"I'm wearing my dinner," said Noob. Yanker laughed. Reid knew it wasn't real—it was one of three randomized laughs that all female ord had—but it still made him smile.

"Don't not eat on account of me," she told him. "We've got a long night of gaming ahead of us. Order a pizza or something."

Reid had the not yet spoiled remains of his anniversary dinner on hand. "I've got some brie and Borodinsky—it's a Russian rye, very thick."

"You like brie?"

"Not particularly. But it's the only cheese higher rent than cheddar that Astrid will eat."

"Shame," said Yanker. "I like a good bucheron or neufechtel myself. Gruyere, too."

Noob perked up. "You like French cheese?"

"As long as the wine's right. But Gruyere's Swiss, not French."

"I knew that." Did he know that? "Okay, who are you? How does someone else actually care about cheeses?"

She shrugged. "I only learned about cheeses because I figure a bottle of wine a night on its own doesn't end anywhere good."

"Whoa, really? Every night."

"Yes, *Mom*. Well, most of one, usually. The opened bottles only keep for so long, so there's usually a few I can grab from the kitchen at the end of my shift. They'd just pour them out otherwise."

"So, wine and gaming?"

"Mm hm. I was near the dregs that night I helped you out. Must have softened me up."

"How far along are you now?"

"Third of a bottle left. Plenty more for dragon watching."

"Fair enough," said Noob. "Yeah. So... what are your thoughts on muenster?"

They chatted long into the night, the dragon all but forgotten.

7

The Fine Art of Power Leveling

*TIP: Grouping with other players is a great way
to earn experience points!*

"Are you sure you don't need any help?" Noob asked again
as the spike-wheeled steamroller ran over Yanker. The criminals driving it cheered.

"I'm good, thanks."

"You look like a bloody waffle."

"It does set damage, not percentile." She popped back up
after the steamroller had passed and shot the driver in the back
of the head.

A burst of light, and Noob leveled. The number above his
head ticked over to 24. *Almost a quarter of the way there.*

He'd hit twenty shortly after they'd entered the Marrowstone
Underground dungeon. Not that he'd contributed much to his
sudden gain in experience points. On Yanker's orders, he stood
in the back while she macheted her way through a horde of
Level 20-25 attackers.

"I just feel like I should be contributing."

"It's faster if you just let me kill everything."

"I can stealth. I do double damage when I backstab. I can halve an elite if I catch him unawares."

"And when you're 100, that'll be key to our damage rotation." She fired a bomb arrow into a cluster of smugglers. Eyepatches and contraband flew everywhere. Because he and Yanker were grouped, Noob got half the experience credit for her kills. "Right now? Just let me play howitzer."

She kicked open the door the smugglers had been guarding and strode into the final zone of the dungeon.

In the narrative, these smugglers were the bane of Marrowstone City. The way the quest givers told it, the Cult of the Underlord was best mentioned only in furtive whispers and innuendo. Three of the NPCs Noob had spoken to had been assassinated by cultists immediately after he'd accepted their quests. They were tough, too—Yanker made him fight those one-on-one, and he'd barely survived.

In the middle of the final room was what players had colloquially dubbed the Suicide Gong. If a toon stumbled into it, or if one of the guards got to it and rang it during combat, the garrisons of all ten of the towers surrounding the chamber would pour into the room and hack your party to bits. "Players *hate* this part," Yanker had told him. "Hate hate *hate* it." If the gong got rung, a total party wipe was the norm.

Yanker drew back her bow. "Never do this, by the way," she said, and fired a shot into the gong.

A horde of enraged smuggler-cultists poured into the room and attacked Yanker. She exchanged her bow for her sword. They fell on her in a ruck, and Yanker switched to cuisinart mode. Limbs and blood fountained out.

"Look, are you absolutely sure you don't need any help?"

"Seriously, I'm fine." Noob couldn't see her through the

106

knot of mutilated smugglers.

"Didn't these guys kill the Chief Marshal?" That was the guy who had commanded Noob to track down and slay the cultists' leader with four of his friends, preferably along a healer / tank / 3x dps split.

"Yep!" Yanker leapt on top of the gong, shedding clumps of dead cultists. The surviving guards stabbed at her without effect; damage calibrated to hurt someone in their twenties lost a bit of its edge seventy-plus levels up.

"They nearly shut down trade with the other Kingdoms of Order." She backflipped back into the fray. "And any martial forces sent into the sewers to clean them out wound up butchered."

Noob kicked his heels against the crate of stolen goods he was sitting on. "Maybe I'm missing something," he said, "but if these guys had the king quaking in his king-boots, and are, to quote the Trademaster General—this is before that assassin set him on fire with that incendiary arrow, which was pretty cool, I have to admit—"

"Yeah, *love* that part," said Yanker. "People will hang around to watch that bit."

"He called them, 'the greatest threat Marrowstone faces today.' So I guess I just supposed this would be, you know…" He indicated the trail of dead criminals stretching behind Yanker like a collapsed conga line. "Harder?"

Yanker wiped dead smuggler off her blade. "The Marrowstone Underground is a low-mid level dungeon, meant to be run by a five-player team of toons at your level. For them, it's a righteous challenge. For me? It's an XP mine for a low level guildie. You've been looting the bodies while you complain, right?"

Noob took in the dozens of unlooted glowing corpses. "I…
uh… "

"Well, then get started while I kill the boss. There's drops
in here that fetch a good price at the auction house." She lit the
four incense sticks around the pentagram in the back of the
room. "And stay back. This guy can be a doozy."

The room darkened. Tendrils of blood red smoke swirled
around the pentagram. **"So,"** intoned a deep and mocking
voice, **"the fools above have discovered our little secret…"**

The winds howled together, forming a freakishly tall being of smoke and blackened bone. His name erupted in flames
above his leering skull: Mort Hyrkanium.

Yanker shot him in the face. Hyrkanium collapsed like a
tower of popsicle sticks.

Noob hit 25 in a burst of light.

"Whoo!" yelled Yanker. "One-shot!" She did a victory
dance.

"A secret you will take to your grave!"

"He's still talking?" asked Noob.

"That's his fight dialogue," said Yanker. "The whole thing
plays no matter how long the fight takes. It can take lowbies ten
minutes to kill this guy."

"You *dare* desecrate this shrine?"

Yanker knelt by Hyrkanium's corpse. "Hey, arrow-face!
Will Death be mocked?"

"Death will not be mocked!"

"Is he hungry? I'll bet he's hungry."

**"You shall all feed His eternal hunger… for *souls!* Mua
ha ha ha HAAA!!!"**

"The writing's not great in this part," Yanker explained.
"They were in a rush to hit beta, and a lot of temp dialogue got
left in."

"You sure know a lot about the company."

She shrugged. "Research. I've read a lot about the game. Gotta know all about them if I'm going to work for them someday."

"**NO!**" yelled Hyrkanium's voice, suddenly panicked. "**It cannot be!**"

"And that would be his death dialogue catching up."

"**I have failed you, master!**" There was groaning and gurgling, and the corpse started to glow.

"Alright, let's see what Satan Claus brought for us." Yanker knelt by the body. "Don't get excited if it's the dagger—that's meant for casters. If it's the boots, then you're in—oh, *now* you drop the gloves? Seventy levels after I need them? Figures." She kicked the body and closed the treasure menu. "Bastard."

"I'm confused," said Noob.

"Well, try to catch up. You're a quarter of the way there. And—" she peered around him at the line of corpses—"you've got a shit-ton of looting to do."

Noob sighed and got to work.

Reid watched Habermann read his progress report with the speed of someone not really reading it. He looked to Reid's sleep-starved brain like a quest giver—mindless and immobile, waiting to dole out the next round of pointless tasks.

Reid noticed Habermann was looking at him quizzically. In a panic, he realized Habermann must have been talking to him. That was definitely his waiting-for-a-reply face. "Uh..." Reid tried, "Yes."

Habermann nodded. "Good. After your accident, I was a bit concerned. Glad to hear next Thursday will work. Actually, let's make it due next Wednesday. Thursday I'll only be here until noon. That won't be a problem?"

Reid sighed internally and shook his head. He had managed to get through the first column of boxes, but that had taken two weeks. Either Habermann hadn't read that part of the report, or he had chosen to ignore it.

How far behind would he have to be for his boss to assign a couple interns to the project?

Habermann was looking at him again. *Shit. I hope he didn't say anything important. He's waiting for a response again. And he's frowning.* "No," Reid guessed.

His boss grinned. "Fantastic. That's what I wanted to hear. The interns are busy enough as it is."

Reid threw up in his mouth a bit.

Habermann saw him gag. "Are you sure you're alright? You're not sick, are you?"

"I haven't been getting much sleep lately," admitted Reid. Actually, the only sleep he'd gotten this week had been on the bus to and from work. He'd slept through his stop that morning and had to ride the entire circuit again to get back to work. "Some new neighbors have moved in. They're up all night."

"You're not contagious? We can't afford for the rest of the office to get sick."

"I was. We were fighting a plaguelord and he hit me with Tomb Rot."

Habermann nodded slowly. "That sounds bad."

"Oh, it was awful. He had a Staff of Corruption. But our healer dispelled the effect, and we killed him, so it was all good."

"So… not contagious?"

"Right as rain." Reid saluted, went back to the mound of work in the conference room, and fell asleep with his head in a file drawer.

Noob hit Level 33 killing a wolf on a picturesque ledge overlooking the sea. The wolf howled and fell still atop a heap of thirty dead packmates.

"Grats," said Yanker. "Two-thirds to go."

Noob knelt to check the wolf and swore. "No liver in this one either."

"We'll just keep grinding." Yanker shot another wolf on the plain below them. The beast streaked towards her, all fangs and fury. Noob stabbed it in the back and found a couple of dead rabbits in the treasure menu.

"We'll get there," Yanker sighed, drawing back her bowstring. "Only need three more."

"How exactly are all these wolves surviving without livers?"

"Their drop rates are just low. Like twenty percent." Yanker shot another. It murder-charged her and died on Noob's dagger—a wicked looking thing he'd found on their run through the Inverted Volcano.

"That's still eighty percent of the wolf population born without a vital organ," Noob pointed out.

"You can't think of it in those terms. Logic sometimes has to take a back seat to mechanics."

"I'll say. Try eating an all meat diet without something to emulsify lipids."

"Look, the quest is asking for 'intact' wolf livers, so we can assume that any wolf that *doesn't* drop one got it damaged when we killed it."

Another wolf charged. Noob Pickpocketed it and came away with its liver. "Got one! Wanna explain how it's still attacking me? And how I just stole an organ?"

Yanker dropped the wolf with an arrow. "You're ruining my immersion."

"It's also got a magic axe." Noob was looting the body. "And chainmail leggings. Wouldn't these have slowed it down?"

"*Immersion.*"

Noob nudged the mound of wolf corpses over the ledge. "As much as I love harvesting wolf guts, aren't dungeons better for power leveling?"

"Yes, but you're in the mid-thirties doldrums. No good dungeons in your breadbasket, not for few more levels. And you've gotta find a drop quest here anyway to even get into the next dungeon. So for the time being, we're grinding XP the old-fashioned way."

"You know wolf livers go for 3,000 gold on the Black Market."

"That's because everyone hates this quest."

"Their hatred is justified."

"Hey, don't be that way. It's a quest to save that sick little girl, remember? If we don't get enough wolf livers, her mom can't make the folk medicine to save her."

"Folk medicine. In a world with magical healing and resurrection. And wolves with axes."

"Immersion." She fired a dozen arrows at a dozen different targets. "Hey, look! Wolves!"

When the frenzied stabbing had ceased, Noob found only a single wolf liver, alongside eight dead rabbits, six wolf flank steaks, five damaged wolf hides, two wheels of cheese, a +2 breastplate vs. chaos damage, and a small scroll.

"'Suspicious letter,'" Noob read off the scroll. "It says, 'This item starts a quest.'"

"Drop quest," said Yanker. "Finally. Now we can get into the Clockwork Abyss dungeon and get the hell out of wolf town."

"What about the little girl?"

"Potions of resurrection are cheap. And we've got four wolf livers to sell on the Black Market."

"Well, what am I supposed to do with all of these wolf steaks?"

Noob hit 40 baking wolf pot pies in the kitchen at Drunkfucker's. The inn had gotten its nickname for the glitch that made its NPC proprietor wobble and fall down at random intervals. Boy Howdy had fixed the glitch in a patch, but the player outcry was so great that they'd reinserted it, and even timed it with appropriate bursts of dialogue.

Yanker had sent Noob to the kitchen when she found out he'd been neglecting his Cookery skill. He would have kept doing so ("I don't see how knowing how to poach a salmon will make me a better backstabber," he'd protested), but Yanker pointed out that he'd ignored his non-combat skills for so long that even basic recipes awarded max XP. So the guild had dumped all of their collective saved meat onto him ("Do you want more of my meat?" Mansex had asked about seventy times) and sent him into the kitchen.

After an hour of cooking, Noob backed out of the kitchen and dropped several thousand XP worth of dishes on the guild's table. "Grub's up. Come taste the fruits of my labor, none of which involve actual fruit."

No one responded. They were stomping and clapping with a hundred other patrons crowded around the fireside table. Noob slipped between toons and spotted Mansex dancing atop it in her skivvies.

"Oh, hey," said Yanker, waving a frothing beer stein. "Didn't see you come in."

Noob folded his arms and sniffed. "I'm not gonna pretend I'm not a little bit offended."

"Gods *damn* it!" the innkeeper blurted as he fell over onto a coat rack.

"Oh, come off it. We got bored waiting, so Mansex put on a show. Bandy dared her to."

"I did no such thing," Bandaid sniffed. "I may have insinuated she was afraid to display her wares in public, but I never *dared* her."

A dwarf tucked a gold goblet in the band of Mansex's panties. She polished his bald head with a kiss.

"I finished off the wolf flanks and basilisk cutlets. Can we go back to adventuring now?"

"Depends," replied Yanker. "What level are you?"

Noob pointed at the 40 above his head.

"And what level do you need to be to enter the Labyrinth of Lost Souls?"

"41," said Bandaid, munching. "Mmm. Good braised unicorn." A +20 Wisdom buff popped up over her head. "Effective, too."

"Forty-one," echoed Yanker. "Which means back to the kitchens, cook-boy."

"Can I at least take off the chef's hat?"

"The one that gives you a 10% XP bonus? That would be a no."

The innkeeper hit the floor. "Blasted pygmies!"

Noob sighed. Then he leveled in a flash of light.

"Well," said Yanker. "That was quick."

"My naga noodle soup must be done."

Bandaid wrinkled her nose. "I never cared for that dish. Too snakey."

Yanker nodded. "Let's get to it, then. Truth, collect Mansex. And Noob, ditch that stupid hat."

The guild crouched behind the only pillar still standing in the ruined throne room as a cackling wizard hurled bolts of black lightning their way, shearing off half the pillar and spattering the guild with plasma-hot shrapnel for thousands of points of damage.

"Take your time, Noob!" yelled Mansex. "I'm basically wearing a bikini here. It offers tons of protection."

Noob was stealthing up behind the wizard. "He's way higher level than me. Are you sure I can take him?"

"No," said Mansex. "You can't take him. That's why the rest of us are here, getting showered with shards of molten pillar. Which does percentile damage. So please kill his ass before we all die. You're making The Truth mad." The Truth shrugged.

Another bolt of lightning. The guild took 15% damage. Yanker glared around the pillar at where she thought Noob was. "Please stab him now."

Noob plunged his dagger into the Wizard's back. As with any action other than walking, the attack broke his stealth.

The wizard whirled on Noob, unhinged his snakelike jaws, and bit at him. His teeth bounced off Bandaid's bubble shield. Then Mansex and Yanker hit him with a fireball and bomb arrow at the same time, and the wizard exploded like a piñata filled with motor oil and roaches.

When Noob presented the wizard's head to the queen, he leveled to 60 in a flash of light.

Noob had nearly finished level 79 when they completed the Hulks. That had been his favorite dungeon yet: a series of sunken shipwrecks haunted by their zombie crews and some feral merfolk who'd taken up residence in the debris.

"How are we even talking?" Noob had asked. They were hovering underwater in the last of the Hulks. "Let alone breathing?"

"Waterlungs enchantments," replied Bandaid. She cast her bubble shield around The Truth as he swam up to skewer one of the merfolk spearmen.

"I'll accept that, but how are Sexy's fireballs working? Explain the physics behind that."

Mansex fireballed a trio of mermaid spellcasters into strips of smoked salmon. "Magic. Now shut up. Please. You're ruining immersion."

"We're immersed right now. That's my exact point."

Noob dropped his protests because the dungeon *was* pretty cool. The final boss was one of the zombie captains, who'd somehow managed to enslave himself a kraken. They fought him in the broken-hulled hold of a galleon perched on the edge of an abyssal trench. The boss rode around on squid-back, stomping holes in the bottom of the ship, and anyone who swam above one of those would get sucked into the inky blackness by the undertow. It patently defied the laws of physics, but it passed the Rule of Cool, so nobody complained. They chopped the boss and his pet into calamari.

Now they were trudging back to shore, dragging a bunch of kraken tentacles behind them. "They make the best thief's gloves," explained Yanker. "All the suction cups, you see. It'll super pump your Pickpocket skill." She stopped to pour the water out of her boots. "Sorry you didn't hit 80. I was sure we'd timed it right."

"No worries." Noob poured the last of the deep sea out of the tricorn hat he'd taken off a mini-boss. "I'm in this for the long haul."

"I know this is taking forever."

"Stuff's been getting harder," Reid admitted. They'd needed the full guild for the last couple dungeons, which meant he got less of the divided XP.

"Yeah, I know, but — I dunno, I can't stop worrying. Like we should have gotten you there by now, and there's so little time. You must be so sick of us."

"You guys aren't that bad. Mansex is, but the rest of you are pretty pleasant people."

"You're just jealous I have an ass that won't quit," said Mansex. "Hey, you think I can make a dress out of all these mermaid scalps?"

"Ah, speaking of that…" Noob reached into his knapsack.

Yanker raised an eyebrow. "If you pull out Ariel's hair, I'm screaming."

Reid opened a trade window between them, dropped a parcel into it. She eyed him suspiciously. "Go on," he told her.

Yanker double clicked on it. Her armor vanished, replaced by a crystalline ball gown that shone in a spectrum of icy colors. A quintet of adventurers jogging down the beach towards the Hulks stopped to whistle.

"It dropped off the zombie bosun down below," said Noob.

"Not really my style," said Yanker, "but it's nice."

Bandaid ogled at the dress. "The Crystalline Dress. One of the rarest treasures of the deep, lost when the Hulks first went under!"

"To translate that into Non-RP Freak," said Mansex.

"That's a super rare drop. You know that goes for about 8k on the market, right?"

Yanker's eyes widened. "I had no idea. I need to start paying attention to deco prices. Noob, this is too much."

Noob shrugged. "Didn't know. Don't really care. It's not real money."

"There are gold farmers in China who'd disagree with you." The dress vanished, her armor appearing in its place. "I'll keep this in a very safe place. Here, I've got one for you."

A trade window opened between them. A parcel appeared inside.

"It's not exactly the same value, but a gift for a gift, right?"

Reid clicked on the package. He found his armor replaced with lederhosen and a Peter Pan cap.

The rest of the quintet, which had whistled before, catcalled and howled. Noob broke into Mansex's sexy dance. Bandaid laughed so hard she fell into the ocean.

Noob hit 80 six minutes later when he killed a Cyclops. He was still wearing the lederhosen.

The final battle with the sky pirates was a tough one. Debates raged on the forums whether this or the Moonhollow on legendary was the (proportionally) hardest dungeon in the game. Reid had read up on it the night before at Yanker's request.

After you destroyed the pirates' base on the crashed floating island (the island *had* been a floating island some time ago, Bandaid explained; before the lore of the game began, it crashed into the top of a mountain, and from a distance it looked like the mountain was wearing a big stone sombrero), the sky pirates fled in their armada of captured ord airships. The final battle took place in the mothership with all of the sky pirate lieutenants rather than a single big boss—a team battle on both sides rather than a tank-and-spank.

That wasn't what made Sky Pirates so deadly, even for level-capped players. The real trouble was the pilot, who would randomly jerk the ship's wheel right or left during the fight. Any players without good footing were likely to fall out of the many ridiculous openings on the flight deck. The lieutenants never fell, of course. And because the ground below was well outside the dungeon, rezzing anyone in the airship who fell out wasn't possible.

Of course, all that was moot if you had a rogue maxed for infiltration.

Noob stealthed between the lieutenants and smacked the pilot with his sap, knocking him cold.

That broke Noob's stealth. The lieutenants all shouted and whirled on him, but Mansex froze them in place with ice blasts.

Noob waltzed from one lieutenant to the next, stunning them with his sap. The Truth followed, kicking each stunned, frozen pirate out an opening.

"Nicely done." Yanker nocked an arrow. "Get ready for round two."

The next hardest thing about Sky Pirates was the reinforcements. After you cleared the flight deck of the mothership, Reid had read, the other airships closed in and swarmed your ship. They dumped more combatants in in waves, and with them came more pilots, who'd pick up with the wheel-jerking where the first had left off.

"Dunno if I have time," said Noob. "I've got work in 45 minutes."

"Plenty of time," said Yanker. "Man the ship's wheel, Lieutenant Noob."

Noob raised an eyebrow. "Why? Don't tell me I can—"

"The wheel, Ensign Noob. I just demoted you for insubordination."

"Aye, Captain." Noob took the wheel.

"Now use Sabotage."

He didn't see anything to sabotage, but he clicked the ability anyway. A HUD for the ship's cannons sprung up. "Whoa."

"There's a reason I had you max your talents on the sneaky shit."

"And here I am without my popcorn," said Mansex.

Yanker grinned wickedly. "Fire at will."

Noob shot down the half dozen airships converging on them. Blimps Hindenberged into the mountains all around them in spectacular blasts of FX.

Noob leveled twice in successive bursts of light. He looked a question at the guild.

"That would be an airship's worth of XP hitting you all at once," said Yanker.

The guild gathered around one of the openings to watch. Three of the burning airships converged to crash into a jagged peak below. The explosion was like the birth of a new star. Noob leveled three more times.

"So much destruction," Mansex purred. She slid her arm around Noob's waist. "So many explosions. So much *death*. More than a girl can take. You deserve a reward."

She started a standing lap dance of sorts, grinding against Noob.

"Uh—" Noob tried not to look at Yanker. "Would you stop that, please?"

"Stay with me," cooed Mansex. "I'm almost there."

The Truth kicked her out a window. She vanished into the distance, both middle fingers raised to the airship.

"Huh," said Yanker. "Didn't know there was a double middle finger macro."

Noob hit 94 before Mansex hit the ground.

The guild apologized in advance for taking Noob into the boss fight at the end of the Risen Pyramid. It was a bad match-up for their group, but he needed the XP. For the best shot at success, and because of all the undead, you wanted to take in a paladin as well as a healer. The pally could alternate fighting with off-healing while the healer dealt the main heals; turning undead *and* healing *and* shielding was just too much for one player. But with Reid dancing on the far edge of 99, they decided (over Mansex's objections) that it was worth the risk.

Five wipes later, they'd changed their tune.

"I'm out of mana," Bandaid whined.

"We know," said Mansex. "We're all at half health."

The Truth pulled his sword out of the last of the latest wave of mummies and struck a defensive stance in front of the gigantic onyx pharaoh's head embedded in the wall of the dungeon's final room. Bandaid took up position behind The Truth.

A slit of blinding light split the head from crown to chin. With a rumble, the great onyx door began to open.

Noob drank a healing potion. "Okay, what do we want to try this time?"

"How about not dying?" suggested Mansex.

Yanker shrugged. "Try to keep them away from Bandy until her mana fills." She checked her quiver. "Great. Out of bomb arrows."

That wasn't good. The boss was Ulix the bony golden-faced fucker who'd killed them five times already. Fighting him was maddeningly frustrating. He'd warp away the split second before you hit him in melee, so the only reliable way to land a blow on him was with a ranged weapon—not a spell, at least not one with more than an instant casting time, because he'd do his blink trick and the spell would miss. Worst yet, before he attacked he'd possess a member of the party, turning them on the other Pwnies and burning through their mana and supplies.

Noob peered into Yanker's quiver. "What have you got left?"

"Glues, icers, and flares. Oh, and a whistler."

"Whoop de shit," said Mansex. "See you in the Underworld. Try to die near the stairs this time. We won't aggro any patrols if we rez there."

The hold spell hit all of them at the same time, just as it had the five times before. They didn't even try to fight it.

Ulix strode out of the great onyx head. "We shall live again," he said calmly, and began to cast. Black plasma flew around his hands.

"Place your bets now," said Mansex. "Who's the traitor this time? My money's on Yanker."

"You should hope it's me. I won't do as much damage. Haven't got the arrows."

Ulix's eyes flared. "We shall live *forever!*"

The Eternal Emperor hurled his spell. The Truth jerked and metamorphosed into a spiny ghoul. He spun on Bandaid.

"It would appear I chose the wrong place to stand," said Bandaid. The possessed Truth cut her in half.

With a grating scream, the hold spell released. Ulix summoned a horde of Egyptian-themed zombies. Mansex machine-gunned fireballs into Ulix until the Truth-ghoul cut her to pieces.

Noob sighed. They were gonna wipe. "Let's go die by the stairs." The Truth-ghoul charged him.

Yanker whipped out her glue arrow. "Noob, do you trust me?"

"Of course."

"Then run for Ulix."

"You'll miss."

"I'm not aiming for him."

Noob ran. The Truth swung at him as he passed; Noob tucked and tumbled under the sword, sprang up, and made for Ulix. The Truth-ghoul whirled after him.

Ulix, true to his programming, backtracked in preparation to blink away. Noob had him cornered, and as he couldn't blink back through a wall, Ulix shot back the other direction— *behind* Noob, into the area The Truth was charging through.

Yanker fired. The glue arrow burst all over the Truth-ghoul and caught Ulix in the radius.

"*Yes!*" Yanker pumped a fist. "Got him! Noob, I think you can take it from here."

Noob wall-jumped out of the corner, flipped, and drove his blade into Ulix's back. The complexity of the maneuver triggered a style bonus, and he critted for 4x regular damage.

The crit broke Ulix's spell. The Truth-ghoul reverted back to The Truth with the dungeon's end boss—the single hardest boss in the game before the expansions were released—stuck to his chest. The Truth's whole body seemed to grin.

Noob hit 100 as Ulix's head bounced down the stairs.

8
Graduation Day

TIP: If another player is harassing you,
you can block them or report them to an Admin.

The Roaring Heart, in the Shady Quarter of Marrowstone City, had gotten its name from its roaring fireplace, now blocked by a legion of dancers. The moment <Pwny Xpress> walked in, Mansex yelled "Oh, hell yeah!" and stripped down to join them. Reid noted that Mansex's default underwear actually covered more of her character than her clothes.

"We're celebrating IRL tonight too," said Yanker, "so everyone drink."

Mansex gyrated between dwarves. "Bandaid!" she yelled. "Get those hot priestly peaches up here!"

"Get behind me, Satan."

"Shake them asses to the masses!"

"That doesn't even make sense."

"Come on, just this once! Show me the wickedness of my ways! It's Noob's birthday, cut loose a little."

"I am a bastion of morality and temperance, a bulwark against temptation."

The bulwark fell after the third round of drinks. A few ciders in, Bandaid was dancing on the table, naked but for her gloves and mitre, hurling buffs and heals at random players.

"That," said Yanker from the guild's table, "is something I never thought I'd see. Or you at the level cap, either," she said to Noob. "And with a day to spare, even!"

Noob put on a smile. "I am very, very tired. And I didn't do it alone. Not by a long shot."

She nodded. "Still quite a feat. Didn't know if you'd make it. Some of us didn't think you would."

"She means me!" yelled Mansex.

"You are one dedicated guy," said Yanker.

Noob shrugged. "Well, with the right girl pushing me..."

The Truth nudged Yanker. "Right! So hey, we got you something. A little graduation present."

A trade window opened in front of Noob. Reid saw a full set of epic-tier armor in it: boots, leggings, *everything*. It was a masterwork of crafted leather, deep violet with gold and silver filigree. A dragon design started at one wrist and swirled up the arm and across the chest.

He'd heard of this set on rogue forums. A player who found even one piece of it was lucky. A full set, with the completion bonuses? People paid real money—good money—out of game to get this armor.

"Purple Ninja Armor," Reid said with reverence. "A full set?"

"The best stealth armor in the game. *World!*" said Bandaid. "I meant world." She plopped down at the table, still in her underwear. "May it aid you in your romantic quest."

"We saved until we had a complete set," said Yanker. "Already had a couple pieces sitting there in the guild bank."

126

"I wanted to sell it," said Mansex.

"So I had these three farming the rest of the drops while you were leveling," Yanker said. "Well? You gonna try it on?"

Reid didn't hesitate. Noob's old billowy black ensemble disappeared, leaving him in his boxers. Piece by piece, the Purple Ninja Armor appeared on his body, culminating with the headpiece. The guild applauded.

"You look awesome," said Yanker.

"I look like a Power Ranger," said Noob.

"It increases your stealth speed by 300% and reduces your Shadowflash cooldown to ten seconds. You can almost sprint in it and stay hidden. You still break stealth when you take an action, but with that rating? Shit, you could sneak up behind a rogue of your own level and not get noticed. Probably steal his pants right off him." Yanker beamed.

Reid didn't know what to say. "This is too much."

"Nah," said Mansex. "Anyone can get the armor with enough effort. The Godsword, though? Only one of those." She chugged half a bottle of whiskey and hurled the rest in the fire. It exploded and set the nearest dancers ablaze. "Well, this has been fun, but I've got lab in the morning. Too bad I'm not Chuck Norris, because—"

"Chuck Norris doesn't sleep," said Noob, over the screams of the burning players. "We've heard it."

"Many, many times," added Yanker. Bandaid extinguished the flames and started handing out heal spells to burnt revelers.

"Yeah, well," said Mansex. "Still true. Night, pigfuckers." She sat and faded away.

"Methinks I too should retire," said Bandaid. "I have much atoning to do for tonight's debauchery. Rest well, noble friends. The Godsword is ours tomorrow."

Her clothes reappeared before she sat and faded from sight.

The Truth clapped Yanker and Noob on the shoulders. Then he, too, sat and vanished.

"It is pretty late," said Noob. "Nearly 2:00am my time."

Yanker nodded. "Yeah."

"I've got work in a few hours."

"Same."

"We should probably go."

"Probably." That would be the responsible thing to do.

Reid wondered what he was doing taking a midnight stroll with a girl whose name he didn't know, whose voice he'd never heard. *Not even a girl,* he reminded himself, *an image of a girl. I have* no idea *who's on the other side of that toon. Not really.*

What worried him wasn't that he was debating whether this was some form of emotional cheating or a strategy to bring Astrid home. What worried him was that after having been alone and miserable for three weeks, with way too much work waiting for him at the office, there was nowhere in the world — real or in-game — he'd rather be than walking beside Mirror Lake with Yanker.

She was laughing. It was the second of the three preset female ord laughs, the one with the sigh at the end. "Can I just say how proud I am of you right now?" she said.

"Thanks? Are you, uh… into your cups tonight?"

"Fifth glass of Que Sera syrah. It tastes terrible, but it pairs really well with 'I don't give a fuck.' Whee!"

"I'm amazed you can even walk straight."

"I think I can handle pressing the one arrow key." She failed to turn with the road and fell off the levy.

"You need a hand?"

"I'm good." A trio of lowbies stopped fishing to applaud her swim back around to shore. "Anyway," she picked up, "you've come a long way, and congrats. Oh, man—you didn't ditch the Purple Ninja hood, did you?"

"No, I just disabled 'show helm' on the options menu. It was weird not being able to see my own head. And there's *tonight's* sentence I never thought I'd say."

She laughed again. It was the first laugh, the one that ended with a tiny, higher register aftershock laugh. That was his favorite.

"That explains it. Sorry, what were we talking about?"

"You were complimenting me on my unlikely ascension."

"Did I tell you how damn sexy you look in that armor?"

"Not really," said Reid. This was veering toward the uncomfortable. Might as well jump in with both feet. "And please, if there's a head-turner here, it's you."

"Aw," said Yanker, kicking a stone into the water. "You'd be disappointed if you saw me in real life."

"Are you kidding?" said Reid. *What am I doing?* "I'll bet you're just as cute in person."

She didn't say anything. They walked on in silence after the levy ended, past a menagerie of lowbies jumping, fishing, dancing, drowning.

The silence got uncomfortable. Reid felt a surge of panic. *You're tired*, he reassured himself. *She probably is, too. You're misinterpreting things. She probably didn't even see the comment, not with five glasses of wine in her. Just don't do anything to make it worse.*

"I'm Reid, by the way," he said. "Reid Underwood. I figured, you know, we've been playing long enough now to actually—"

"Don't," she said. "I told you. No real names in here."

"Well… why not?" He told himself to shut up, but that had

MATT VANCIL

stung. "What's wrong with knowing who you're playing with? We're on the same team, here, but I don't know anything about you."

She stopped. "I don't want real life in here. This isn't the place for it. This is my escape. My *out*. You were the one bringing reality in, woe is me, have you seen my girlfriend, here's her Social Security Number. Please, no more real life. It's not what I'm here for."

"Clearly."

They sulked a while in silence.

"So you're almost done, yeah?" blurted Yanker. "We find the sword, that's it, you get your girl and you're out?"

"That's the plan. Didn't realize how bad-fairy-tale it sounded until you said it just now." *Whatever.* "I'm ready to get back to real life."

"Not me," said Yanker. "Glass number six." She turned to look out over the lake.

There were two perfect moons that night: the real one that hung enormous in the sky, and the reflection where it touched the rim of the lake. *Bullshit*, thought Reid. *Both moons are fake.*

"I'd spend my whole life in here if I could," Yanker said, still looking out over the water. "Plug me full of food lines, screw a VR helmet to my face, I don't care." She turned to Noob. "Come on, you can't tell me you haven't enjoyed all this."

He didn't want to admit how true that was—that sometimes the fun of the game had eclipsed the motivation of finding Astrid. "It has been fun at times."

"At times? Why do you have such a chip on your shoulder about the game?"

"It's that…" *Don't say it.* Grandpa had warned him, *Never criticize what they love.* Too late, he was typing. "None of this is

130

real! None of it. Those moons, that lake. Those merrows."

A trio of ugly fish-frog monsters burbled out of the lake to attack a lowbie who'd been fishing in their aggro range.

"People are cashing in real life to be here. And for what?" Reid watched the words appear on the screen. "It's not like you can really know anyone in here. Not really. You can pretend to be whatever the hell you want, and no one can check up or call you on it. It's just a really well-rendered version of internet chat. It's depressing."

The lowbie died with a scream in the shallows. The merrows, still aggroed, ran up and started stabbing Noob. He was Level 100, so they only did a fraction of a percentage point of his total health in damage. He ignored them.

Yanker stood still for quite some time before answering. "I still prefer it here."

"To what? I really want to know. Hell, if I knew, I'd know what I'm not giving Astrid. What can you *possibly* get in here that you don't in real life?"

"You're really gonna make me say it, aren't you?"

Noob spread his arms. "Say what?"

"In here, I *matter*." Yanker looked at the ground. Reid imagined pain in her eyes when she looked up at him and said, "Here, I have friends. I have something to offer! I'm good, *really* good. Head of a kickass guild *I* built from the ground up! I have a PVP rating in the tens of thousands. People *see* me here. I *matter* here. I get to have adventures and friends and make legends. Hell, I'm even *pretty*."

"But it isn't real," said Reid in the real world. Noob echoed him as he typed the words in.

"It's real enough," said Yanker. "And I'd rather spend what time I've got on this mudball with people who play make-believe than a bunch of arseholes who don't even care."

"What about the game design thing?" Reid asked. "You can't really do that in here."

"I'm too drunk to pretend I ever even had a chance."

"My God. That's so sad."

"Hey, piss off. Don't you *dare* pity me. You don't know a fucking thing about me!" She stormed off and sat down on the shore of the lake.

"You're right," Noob said. "I don't. But… I'd like to. You're one of the best people I've met." He'd meant in the game when he typed it, but he didn't correct himself. It was true in the broader sense as well. "You're the only one who makes this whole thing bearable, this whole stupid Godsword quest. If you hadn't stopped to help me that night — Bandaid would call it fate, but then again she's crazy — I don't know where I'd be. It certainly wouldn't be here, on the verge of getting my life back. So, you know, I'd like to *thank* you." Reid swallowed. "Not just Yanker. *You.*"

Yanker faded from sight, and was gone.

9
Graveyard of the Gods

TIP: A Boy Howdy employee will never ask for your password.

"How are you doing?" Lodge asked. "Or do I even want to know?"

Reid stretched, shook the cobwebs from his head. He looked around the conference room. "I went for a walk with Yanker last night."

"Please tell me that's not drug lingo."

"The ord ranger girl."

"This is your guild leader?"

"She is."

"And you're *sure* she's a girl."

"Sure I'm sure." Reid frowned. "Why wouldn't I be sure?"

"So you've heard her voice, then."

Reid looked away. "Not exactly." He tried to be subtle as he wiped his drool puddle off the table. "But I will! We're running the grand epic dungeon tonight, and the guild set up a GroupSpeak line so we can communicate without stopping to type."

"So you haven't heard her voice."

"I haven't heard her *speak*, no. But if you mean have I heard her *voice*, as in do I have a sense of her opinions, turns of phrase, that sort of thing—then yes."

"That is absolutely not what I meant."

"We communicate very well," sniffed Reid. "We've got a good rapport going, the kind that only comes with real respect and trust."

"What's her name?"

"She wouldn't tell me."

They heard Habermann coming before he sauntered into the room. By the time he entered, Lodge had dropped to the floor to fiddle with Reid's ethernet connection.

"Good news." Habermann slapped a sweaty stack of folders on the table and indicated the wall of boxes blocking the conference room windows. "By tomorrow, all this will be gone."

Reid brightened. Finally, a bit of luck. He quashed the urge to hug his boss. "Oh, thank you. I was so worried. Any help, even an intern, would be fantastic." Reid stopped when he saw the flat line of Habermann's mouth. "Nobody's joining me?"

Habermann looked like he couldn't tell if Reid were joking. "I'm sorry, but we really can't spare anyone. But your project's been fast tracked. I need this all done by tomorrow noon."

Reid slumped and gaped like a marionette whose operator had just had a heart attack. Habermann mistook it for gratitude and slapped a meaty hand across Reid's back. "Congratulations, Reid! This is the kind of dedication the Board looks for in our young employees. If you wind up spending the night, don't leave the building after 9:00pm or you'll trigger the alarm." He trundled back to his office.

"I could set fire to the building," offered Lodge. "You could escape in the chaos."

Reid shook his head. If the building burned down, he'd be stuck answering questions all night instead of playing.

Once Lodge had left, Reid fell into an easy rhythm. The work was repetitive, but just engaging enough to keep him awake.

He found himself humming as he whirred along, making corrections and signing off on resolved issues. Most of the multi-file boxes turned out to have a summary at the head of each file, and Reid discovered all he had to do was look these over for discrepancies. If the numbers didn't add up, only then did he have to dive into the file and root out the inconsistency. It was the kind of work he could do half-asleep, without conscious thought. He was making great time.

Reid was distantly aware that he'd slipped into a state of *no mind*, that elusive Zen condition of pure, unconscious reaction. His grandmother would have been pleased. She'd given him koans to help him untangle his larger homework projects — nonsense thought puzzles you could only solve if you let them knock you out of rational, linear thought, and when you *did* solve them, the obviousness of the solution punched you right in the face and left you laughing at how much you overthought.

The one that had stuck with him the most was the Muddy Road:

Two monks, Tanzan and Ekido, were walking to the temple through rain so thick it had turned the road to mud. They came upon a young woman in a silk kimono standing by the side of the road, unable to cross. Without hesitation, Tanzan said "Well, come on, then," picked her up, and carried her across the road.

Ekido didn't speak to Tanzan until late into the night. He fumed in silence all the rest of the day until they'd reached their destination. Once they had arrived at the temple, Ekido could contain himself no more.

"Our order forbids us to interact with women!" Ekido shouted at Tanzen. "Especially the young and beautiful ones. It could lead to us breaking our vows! Why on earth would you do that?"

"I left the girl back at the road," Tanzan told Ekido. "Why are you still carrying her?"

Reid signed off on another return. He didn't realize that was the last one until he reached for the next, and there wasn't one. "Well. How about that."

Lodge peered into the room. "Hey."

"Not just yet," said Reid. "I'm so close to done."

"Trust me," said Lodge. "You'll want to make time for this."

Reid glanced at the clock. The numbers were blurry, but he figured he could probably afford a break. "Sure, what is it?"

Astrid stepped in past Lodge. She looked decidedly humble, almost deflated. Her mascara had been running. "Boo-Bear?"

Reid's heart leapt into his throat and carried him to his feet. "Astrid?"

"Hey. It's me. I'm… ah—sorry for leaving. And everything."

Reid rubbed his eyes. She was really there. "Are you okay? I was so worried."

She fumbled off her glasses. "Look, we don't have to do this here, and I don't really want to. I just—" She sniffed her tears back in, wiped her eyes; she hated crying. "I really want to come home, Reid. Can I just come home?"

"Of course." He folded her into his arms. She hugged him back, hard.

Lodge watched them for a moment before closing the door behind him.

Reid dried her cheeks with the cuff of his sleeve. "Don't," she protested. "You'll stain your cuff."

"It's okay."

"It was one of Frank's favorites."

"It'll wash out."

She smiled. God, she was beautiful. She pulled off his glasses and kissed him gently. Lightning arced down Reid's spine, crackling into his toes and sending his heart racing.

He could stop now. He could stop and go home and everything would be exactly the way it had been.

He brushed his lips against hers. With a light moan, she kissed him — hard — almost a bite out of his mouth, and tackled him.

Reid landed on his back on the conference room sofa he hadn't known was there. Astrid straddled him. "Here's something else I've missed," she purred, and reached for his belt.

Reid pulled her hands away. "We can't! Not here. Not at work. It's in the manual."

She smiled coyly. "Oh, we can't, can we?" She ripped open her blouse.

The white of her bra stood out starkly against her dark blue skin. That seemed odd. "Honey?"

Astrid reached under her chin and ripped off her mask. Yanker was perched atop him, an impish smile on her indigo face. She reached for his belt again. "Let's go find your sword, Noob."

Reid jerked awake at the conference table. Someone else in the room yelled, but he couldn't see who it was: a page was drool-glued to his face.

He ripped it off and saw Lodge crouching defensively in the doorway. "You scared the shit out of me."

"Sorry." Reid checked the table. It wasn't the file he'd been working on in the dream. Come to think of it, the file in his dream had been labeled "Last File," which should have been a giveaway.

Reid looked back at the wall of boxes and groaned. He was barely a third of the way in. "Is it one yet? Did I sleep through lunch?"

Lodge pointed at the clock. It was after 6:00pm. "You slept through the day. Good thing Habermann didn't see you."

"Yeah," said Reid. "Lucky, lucky me."

"Do you need a ride home?" Lodge asked.

Reid gestured to the mountain of boxes. "I'm not getting home tonight."

"Don't take this the wrong way, but I'm super glad I don't have the skills to help you."

Reid chuckled. "You'd only slow me down."

"Well, hey, it could be worse. At least you got *some* sleep." Lodge started tugging on his coat. "I could bring you a coffee if you like."

"Should I meet her?" Reid blurted.

Lodge froze, his coat halfway on.

"Yanker," Reid continued. "My guildmaster? I think I want to meet her."

Lodge extracted his arm from the coat. "Wow. Okay." He folded the coat to give himself time to consider his answer. "All right. I'm gonna base my answer on three premises. First one is that she's actually a girl."

"She *is* a girl," Reid said. Reid hoped.

"Second, that she's geographically close, no farther than say a six hour drive. Because a flight to meet somebody who won't tell you her name is beyond the borders of weird."

Reid's face fell. "I hadn't thought of that."

"The weird part, or that she could be anywhere on the globe?"

"Doesn't matter. Forget I said anything."

"Bit late for that. Third premise: the fact that you're asking me this at all means you see this woman as something potentially serious."

"Hey, now, I never said—"

Lodge held up a hand. "I'm just walking through what you've told me—I can only go off the information I've got. So. You say she's nice. You deserve better than nice, but nice is a good start, and it's leagues beyond what you've been getting. You think you don't deserve to be happy, so I won't bring up how you are when you're with Astrid, but I will point out that when you're talking about Mystery Girl—"

"Her name is Yanker." *Except no, it's not. Shut up, brain.* "And when exactly was I talking about her?"

"The ride home from the hospital. You wouldn't shut up about her. You were pretty well sedated at the time, but the whole time you were babbling about her, you weren't panicked. You weren't pretending that everything was perfect like you do with Astrid. You were more... I don't know, *human. Real.* I won't say *happy*, because that was probably the painkillers. But even now, sleep deprived and buried under this mountain of shit work, we're talking about *her.* And you're about as calm as I can remember. It's nice to see you not pulling your hair out because you're not measuring up to some impossible standard you've set for your relationship. So, to summarize: I don't know. Good night, Crotch-Priest."

"Later, Ass… Butt."

Lodge could only shake his head. "Man, you really need to get some rest."

The last of the office workers departed around a quarter to eight. That gave Reid fifteen minutes to get ready.

He filed away the last of what he'd gotten done—three full columns, only six boxes to go—and tucked a picture of Astrid into the edge of his laptop. He pulled his copy of *Fartherall Online* out of his backpack and violated about a dozen rules in the manual by installing it on his office computer.

Once the game had loaded, Reid plugged in a headset from customer service (rule violation #13). "Here we go." He dialed up the guild's GroupSpeak channel and pulled on the headset.

He heard a *ping*, and then staticky silence. "Um… hello?"

"Hello?" The voice was a young woman's. "Noob? Is that you?"

"Reid, yeah. Who is this?"

"Who do you think it is? It's Yanker."

Reid let out a massive sigh. *She* is *a girl. I told you, Lodge.* Relief massaged his brain. But there was something odd about her voice, her… accent? "Yanker?"

"Yeah?"

"You sound Australian."

"I *am* Australian."

Reid didn't know how to parse that. "Why are you Australian?"

"Why *wouldn't* I be?"

Australia. Way out of his time zone—an ocean away. "I'm sorry."

"She'll be apples, mate," she said with a laugh—her real

laugh, not a canned sound file from the game, a long chuckle that ended with a dingo yip of a gasp. "Kidding, sorry. I don't actually talk like that. Nobody talks like that anymore. I'm betting half of that old ANZAC lingo was based a dare: 'How stupid an expression do you think *I* can get to catch on?' Anyways, I babble a bit when I'm nervous. You can tell me to shut up."

Reid didn't say anything. He was still thinking about her goofy laugh.

"You there?" she asked.

"Yeah. It's just…" The picture of Astrid had fallen out of his laptop. He set it back in. *Focus, Reid. Back on track. Goals and shit.* "I just didn't expect you to sound like that." *To have a laugh that sweet. No. Focus.* "Where are you guys?"

"The Graveyard of the Gods, near side of the Bleak Continent."

Above the blasted and preternaturally dark landscape of the Graveyard of the Gods swirled a vortex, an inverted whirlpool of crackling energy and mournful winds. Lightning fell from it like rain. Shattered monuments jutted up from the red sand, surrounded by the detritus of the fallen and forgotten, the flotsam of dead gods and dead worlds dumped unceremoniously onto the ground from the vortex.

Noob found the rest of <Pwny Xpress> waiting for him on the top of a red rock ridge.

Yanker jogged down the hill to meet him. "Cutting it a bit close."

"Hey, I ran halfway across the world for this." Below the ridge, the angry mouth of a temple squatted in the side of a collapsed mountain.

"What is that place?"

"Ord-Anmuhr," said Yanker. "The ancestral home of my people, back when the orcs and the ord were the same race. Then the dwarves took some of us captive, tortured and experimented on us, and blah blah blah, poof, orcs." She grinned. "The only thing that *does* matter," she continued, "is that the Moonchart Door opens in the back of that dungeon. In less than an hour."

"No pressure."

"*All* the pressure. Okay, I'm patching you in to the guild line… now."

"—so the cop says 'Did you know you have a dead cat back here?'" a young man was saying. "'And Shrödinger's like, 'Well, *now* I do.'"

Reid reached the top of the ridge right as a woman replied 'I know not of this "Schrödinger." This is some powerful wizard, I assume?' That was Bandaid. The game matched her toon's speech animation to her player's voice. It was almost like watching a real person talk.

"Ahoy, ahoy!" Noob called to his guild. <Pwny Xpress> turned to greet him.

"Well met, noble sir!" Bandaid clasped his hand and hit him with a health buff that increased his hit points by 10%.

"Nice to hear you in person," he said.

"Whatever do you mean?" she asked. "You've known the sound of my voice since we met."

"It's okay to break character once in a while," said Yanker.

"This expression, 'break character…' does that have something to do with shattering one's will?"

Yanker shook her head. "She's a lost cause."

Bandaid winked.

"All right," said Noob, "I've heard Yanker and Bandaid. So what does Mansex sound like?"

"There's lots of panting," said Mansex—in the man's voice Reid had heard earlier. "And groaning."

"Wait," said Noob. "You're a dude?"

Mansex threw back her hair. No, his. Hers? "Duh."

"You didn't pick up on that?" Yanker asked Noob. "*How*?"

Noob shook his head. "It does explain a lot."

Bandaid wrinkled her face. "I cannot *believe* I danced with you."

Noob turned away from the wizard. "Okay, that's three. Where's The Truth?"

"The Truth doesn't talk," said Yanker. "Thought you'd have picked up on that by now. Enough of the meet and greet. We all have real voices and nobody sounds like what we thought they would. Let's go kill something."

"Right on," said Mansex. "Looks like we've got some competition to get through, too."

"There is?"

The Truth pointed down towards the temple's recessed entrance. An army of rock monsters ("Golems," Bandaid whispered) were patrolling the entrance in tight clusters. Outside the temple, well out of the golems' aggro range, a pair of 50-man raids had squared off. Taunts and the occasional water balloon flew between the groups, but nobody attacked. Yet.

"Methinks ours was not the only guild to complete a Moonchart," said Bandaid.

Yanker nodded. "Looks like Design compensated accordingly. Those golems are ten levels higher than normal."

Below, a player who was tired of waiting or just plain crazy raised his axe and charged the golems, bellowing like a horny

143

gorilla. His raid ran after him. Whether that was to restrain him or join the attack, it didn't matter—the golems converged and pounded the disorganized raid to death in seconds. The other raid cheered and jeered and shot off fireworks.

"I think we can safely cross suicide charge off our tactics list," said Mansex.

Noob stared down at the dead raid. "I must be missing something. If fifty people couldn't get past those golems, how are we supposed to with five? We're outnumbered twenty to one."

"We're not gonna fight," said Yanker, "we're gonna sneak our way in. And by *we*," she turned to Noob, "I mean *you*. You stealth your way past the patrols, find us a clear spot on the inside, and Mansex teleports us to you. Lather, rinse, repeat."

Three Level 100 rogues from the surviving guild apparently had the same idea. They treaded up to the golems' aggro ranges and vanished into stealth. A few seconds later, the golems converged on three separate spots in their ranks and pounded craters into the ground. Dead rogues materialized in each.

"Well, suck," said Noob.

"I wish you had not seen that," said Bandaid.

"Relax," said Yanker. "Those guys didn't have the Purple Ninja Armor."

"Those two did," Mansex pointed out. "See? You can see the purple between the smears of blood."

"You're not helping."

The Truth ruffled Noob's hair. Bandaid cast her shield bubble on him.

Noob dropped into stealth and snuck down the ridge. "Remember!" Mansex called after him. "If at first you don't succeed, you're not Chuck Norris!"

Noob wove his way down the ridge, towards the

golem-patrolled swath in front of the temple, and through the remains of the dead raid. The first of them were just now returning from the Underworld.

The other raid, sensing an opportunity, signaled an attack on the newly revived. Noob dodged and weaved as spells exploded and arrows fell all around him. Someone must have aggroed the golems, because they started buzzing through the warring raids like wasps through bees, leaving a trail of dead players on both sides.

Noob skittered between charging golems. "I'm gonna die."

An orc with two golems chasing him was heading straight for Noob. Noob dropped and rolled. The golems passed so close he could see the cracks and lines in their stony faces. "I'm gonna die."

He hopped up and stealthed past the craters with the dead rogues. "I'm *really* gonna die."

An oddly uniform rumbling made Noob stop and look up. The golems had killed the last members of both raids and had lumbered back to their preset posts. Noob found himself in the heart of their cluster, six golems within lunging distance. He kept absolutely still.

"Where are you, Noob?" Yanker was safely back on the ridge.

"About forty yards from the entrance," he said, "but I can't move. I'm pinned."

"You're stealthed. And maxed for infiltration. They can't see you."

"If you can see Chuck Norris," said Mansex, "he can see you. If you *can't* see Chuck Norris, you're seconds from death."

"Mansex," said Noob, "*the fuck up*: would you *shut it* for me, please?"

The golem nearest Noob began to move, sliding along its patrol path. Noob fell in after it, matching its speed a pace behind.

The golem's patrol track paralleled the entrance to the dungeon entrance. The golem rumbled about twenty yards before abruptly turning and starting back the way it came. Noob darted out of its path and into the wake of a golem heading the other way, and rode that back the way he'd come. Twenty yards in the other direction, he jumped to another, and followed this pattern through the mob, stealthing behind the patrols row after row, until he passed the last one and stood before the yawning gate.

"I'm through!" he yelled. His guild cheered. It was the second time anyone had cheered him. It was a hundred times less loud than when he made the shot, but it meant about a hundred times more to him.

"I'm through!" Noob stealthed through the gaping entrance into the temple proper, where the ceiling soared high above the floor. "I'm... !" Of course the ceiling was high—it had to be, to make room for the 50-foot tall titans patrolling just inside the entrance.

Noob was so startled to see the titans that he failed to notice the wall of electrical current until he'd stepped through it. The wall did minimal damage, but enough to his stealth.

As one, the titans glared down at him. "I'm toast."

The nearest titan punted Noob with a horse-sized foot. Noob crunched into the ceiling with bone-pulverizing force.

Noob couldn't hear sound of the Reaper over the battle. The ghosts of the raids had carried their grudge into the Underworld. Ghosts killed ghosts, and when one died, its ghost—*a ghost of a ghost; how does that even work?*—popped out of the ghost corpse and rejoined the fight.

It was fun to watch. Noob kicked back and enjoyed the show until a column of light shone down over him.

Noob stepped out of the column of light Bandaid had called down from the heavens. He was back on the ridge with the rest of the guild. "Titans," he reported. "Ten of them, maybe more. And there's a thin lightning wall inside to break stealth."

"Titans are not part of this dungeon," said Bandaid. "They never have been."

"Neither's the lightning wall," said Mansex. "Design over-compensated. No wonder no one's gotten through."

"Don't want to sound pessimistic, but this is bad," said Yanker. "The door opens in half an hour. We miss it, we have to wait another month."

"And find a new Moonchart," added Bandaid.

"No way," said Noob. "I won't survive another month of this." He scanned the temple from the ridge.

The way in looked hopeless. A third raid had shown up, and the golems were busy smashing them to death. Noob looked at the mountain the temple was built into, and noticed a balcony high off the ground. On the balcony there, a patch of black pulsed in a doorway.

Noob whipped out his spyglass and checked. "There's a black circle up there."

Yanker looked where Noob indicated. "That's the dungeon's exit. Where you come out after you kill the end boss."

"It's out of reach," said Mansex. "Way too high. Believe me, people have tried. They make it like that so no one can get in through the back door."

"But that's what it is? A back door?"

Mansex nodded. Noob grinned. Mansex frowed. "What?"

"Those titans," said Noob. "They're punters."

The guild exchanged looks. The Truth got it. His shoulders shook with silent laughter.

While golems chased down raiders below, Noob led Yanker along the knife's edge of a ridge until she had a clear line of sight into the temple. "Do you see them?"

"Yep," she said, looking through his spyglass. "Ten. No, twelve. Level 200. Yeesh. I've never tried kiting anything that big before."

"Do you think it'll work?"

"Only one way to find out." She drew a long-range arrow to her ear and let fly. Her shot vanished into the temple.

"Well? You get him?"

An enraged roar echoed out of the dungeon. "That's a yes. Look out, he's pissed."

The ground shook with each footstep as the titan thundered out of the entrance. It stormed up the ridge in three strides and would have squashed them if Mansex hadn't hit it with an ice bolt. That cut its speed in half—which only made it twice as fast as everyone else.

"Keep it here!" yelled Yanker, pumping arrow after arrow into the giant. "Don't break aggro!"

Noob positioned himself with his back to the balcony in the distance. "Bubble me, Bandy!" The priest cast her shield spell on Noob right as Yanker backpedaled past him, firing up into the titan's knees.

"Now!" yelled Yanker.

Noob backstabbed the titan—well, ankle-stabbed him. The effect was the same. The bot's algorithms calculated the damage it had taken per player per second, identified Noob as the biggest threat, and whirled on him.

"Kick me again, you overgrown pituitary case!" Noob yelled up at him. "Kick me! *Kick me!*"

The titan obliged. The kick shattered Bandaid's shield and knocked Noob's hit points into single digits. Bandaid managed to tag him with a flash heal as he rocketed towards the mountain. He hoped it would be enough. If not, there'd be a Noob-colored stain somewhere in the vicinity of the balcony.

Noob hung in midair for a second at the peak of his arc before plummeting down towards the mountainside. He slammed into the stone wall above the balcony, dropping his hit points back to singles. Reid activated Slowfall, and Noob slid down and flopped onto the balcony.

He leapt to his feet in a celebratory dance. "Made it!"

"Woot!" yelled Yanker. "Sky punt for the win!"

"That was some crazy-ass Chuck Norris kind of awesome!" said Mansex. "Hang on, teeping to your location."

The guild appeared in a flash before Noob and burst into applause and dance.

"You," said Yanker, throwing an arm over his shoulder. "Are *so* misnamed. That was *legend*, that was."

"Well," said Noob, "I had a good teacher." He made an "after you" gesture towards the black circle, and <Pwny Xpress> stepped through the back door of the dungeon.

10
The First God's Tomb

TIP: There is no moon level.

The guild found itself at the end of a short stone hallway. Tapestries of constellations hung from the walls: a jester in motley; a noble queen; a magnificent sword; a monstrous dragon; two lovers entwined.

Bandaid glanced up at the tapestries. "I have no memory of these."

"They're not part of the dungeon," said Mansex. "Must be deco for the Moonchart event."

"Focus," said Yanker. "Keep on the goal. Let's not get distracted. If they put titans at the entrance, they've probably increased the difficulty back here as well."

A grotesque scream came from around the corner. Mansex perked up at it. "Well. At least they haven't changed *that*."

The Truth took point and led them around the corner. Through a vaulted archway in the antechamber beyond, they could see a malformed blue giant trapped in a glass tank. Wires and tubes stuck out of its back. It screamed and pounded against the glass. The dwarf mad scientists studying the giant and the golem guardians paid <Pwny Xpress> no mind—they were well out of aggro range.

"That," said Yanker, "is the final boss of Ord-Anmuhr. We would've had to fight our way past him if we'd gone in through the front. It's pretty cool—he kicks his way out of the tank when you pull aggro and starts whomping arse and it's just utter chaos."

"Yeah, not really gonna miss fighting his blue bulbous ass." Mansex waved at the giant. "Kill ya later, dude."

The giant screamed and pounded.

"What's that?" said Mansex. "Why of course you can kiss my rosy elfin patootie!" He shook her posterior at the giant. It screamed again.

Yanker sighed. "Please don't taunt the hyper-elite mega-boss. Got time for a quick bio break?"

"My hunger is great," said Bandaid. "I shall procure myself a sandwich." She and Yanker went inert.

"And I shall dance." Mansex shucked and jived. The giant screamed.

Noob averted his eyes. "For the love of all that is good and holy, please stop dancing."

"Never!" said Mansex. "Thrill to my sexy!"

Noob was looking away, so he heard rather than saw the golems rumble around the corner. Noob spun around, daggers in hand, as the first golem punched Mansex across the face and knocked her against the far wall.

"Patrol!" yelled Mansex, no longer dancing. "Help!"

The Truth slid in front of Mansex and caught the golem's punch square on his shield. The other two swarmed and pounded on Yanker and Bandaid, who just stood there, motionless, shedding hit points and shaking with damage animations.

Noob hurled a smoke bomb to distract the golems and broke a vial of thundershock over his blade, and leapt to defend his friends—

And the world froze, and went dark.

Reid's screen blacked out. He yelped and slapped the computer. "Hello?" His headset had gone dead—no sound from the game. This couldn't be happening. "Hey! *Guys!*"

The screen kicked to his desktop, where an instant message was waiting for him in his chat program. He mentally slapped himself—*Why didn't I quit that?*—and moused over to shut the window.

RedStar89: Are you there?

Reid just started at the message, trying to place the name.

RedStar89: Boo-Bear?
RedStar89: Hello?

Reid pounced on his keyboard, typed back:

CheeZeus: I'm here! Are you okay?
RedStar89: I really miss you.

He sat there, staring at the message. She *missed* him.

I should feel relieved, he told himself. I should be whooping and hollering and forgetting about everything else. Must be tired. Nothing else should matter right now—not work, not the game…

Reid blinked. Oh, shit. *The game.* He typed:

CheeZeus: I'm with friends, one sec.

And clicked on the *Fartherall Online* tab.

❉ ❉ ❉

Chaos.

Mansex and Yanker lying dead on the floor. The Truth landed a deathblow on a golem and it exploded in a shower of stone.

The other two golems flanked The Truth and pummeled him with massive stone fists. The Truth couldn't move his shield fast enough to block both. His health dropped. Bandaid pumped heal after heal into him, but her mana was running low.

Noob just stood there. Someone was yelling in his ear. Yanker. "—you there? Noob, *help us*—!

Noob snapped to and hurled a knife into the nearest golem's back.

It turned and charged him. The screen froze again—

—and kicked Reid back to his desktop, to another message from Astrid.

RedStar89: I'm still pretty mad at you.

Reid fought down the urge to type the first six things that came to mind. Instead, he replied—

CheeZeus: I know how you feel.

—and clicked back to the game.

On screen, Reid saw Noob lying dead in the dungeon hallway beneath a message: *You have died.* "Oh, that's fair."

RedStar89: Are you even there?

Fear gnawed a hole in Reid's stomach. No need to rush back now, not with the guild dead. Either Bandaid had lived, or she hadn't. If she was dead, that was it for them—they'd have to rez outside the dungeon, and they'd miss their window for the

Moonchart Door.

And why the hell am I thinking about the game? Astrid is right here!
He curled over his keyboard.

> **CheeZeus:** Always. Always here. Are you okay? I miss
> you terribly.
> **RedStar89:** Just REALLY frustrated right now.
> **CheeZeus:** I still know how you feel.
> **RedStar89:** Seriously doubt that.

He checked back in the game. No column of light. Bandaid must be dead. That was it, then.

It was his fault. There was no way a trio—even a level pumped one—should have taken out their five, not if Noob had been there pouring DPS into the patrol instead of pulling a mannequin.

Now he had to explain that he cost them their once-in-a-month shot at the Godsword because his girlfriend chose that exact moment to reinitiate contact. *That'll go over well.*

What would he tell them if she came home? They'd understand if he didn't want to keep playing, right? Of course they would. He'd been up front about that. He had only ever been playing to get Astrid back.

He set his jaw and typed:

> **CheeZeus:** So I started playing Fartherall Online. I'm
> going to get the Godsword.
> **RedStar89:** Come again?

Reid panicked.

> **CheeZeus:** And when I get it, I'm giving it to you. If
> you come home.

155

So much for guild solidarity. They'd understand. He told them at the beginning why he needed the damn thing. What difference would it make if he gave it directly to her instead of the Admin?

> **RedStar89:** What is it with you guys? The Godsword is impossible.
> **CheeZeus:** If I get it for you, will you come home?
> **RedStar89:** You can't even get in the fucking dungeon.
> **CheeZeus:** No, you have to kite one of the titans out and get him to punt you to the balcony.
> **CheeZeus:** Will you PLEASE come home?

He waited for a response. None came.

> **CheeZeus:** Astrid? You still there?
> **CheeZeus:** Hello? I'm on GroupSpeak line 6546419 if you want to chat. My guild's cool, they're nice.
> **CheeZeus:** Most of them.
> **CheeZeus:** I joined a guild by the way.

Still no response. She might have gone.
"Oh, *shi*—" Reid realized what he'd forgotten to ask her.

> **CheeZeus:** WHAT IS YOUR CHARACTER'S NAME?

No response. Reid strangled the air and clicked back on the game tab.

"—couldn't I talk to you? You went dead and disappeared!"

Yanker was yelling through the Underworld.

"I'm here," he said. "I didn't go anywhere." A column of light shone down over Mansex, and she vanished.

"We almost wiped! If Bandaid had died, there'd be no one to rez us!" So Bandaid *had* made it. That was good. "We'd have missed the Moon Door."

"Yeah."

"What happened to you? You just disappeared. You were there, and then you were just gone."

"Sorry," said Noob. "Computer froze."

"It scared me."

"Me, too. We almost lost our shot at the Sword."

"I'm not talking about the Sword! I mean, I *am*, it's just not what I was..." She looked away.

"Then what...?" Noob studied her face.

The column of light shone down over Yanker. Her azure skin lit up in a million tiny rainbows. She regarded Noob quietly.

"It's Jodie," she said, her voice barely a whisper. "My name is Jodie."

The rest came out in a rush. "I live in Noosa Heads. It's a tourist town about a hundred and forty k's from Brisbane."

"Yanker—" Noob caught himself. "Jodie. The others—"

"I took them off the line. Don't know how far that is in miles, sorry. I work nights at a resort front desk and I sell things on eBay. It's not much of a living. But it lets me spend my days in here, where I *do* have a life. Friends. My guild. And you."

Over his headset, Reid heard wine being poured, the foot of a wineglass scraping a desk. She took a sip.

"Please don't disappear again." Yanker looked up into the light. "Okay, Bandy." She vanished. The mists of the

Underworld filled in the gap where she'd been standing.

"Jodie." Reid tried out her name. He liked the way it felt. He pictured a woman in a clerk's outfit, putting on a smile to greet guests, counting down the hours until she could escape her life, throw her uniform in a corner, and come home. His heart ached.

The column of light shone down on him. "It is not yet your time," said the Reaper. "Return to the world, and live again."

Noob rose from column of light in the hallway where he'd died.

Yanker helped him to his feet. "Welcome back." For a fleeting moment Reid wished she'd kept the rest of the guild off the line.

Shattered stone bodies lay scattered around The Truth, who had seated himself and was eating a steak, somehow without removing his helmet. Noob took in the bits of golem all about. "You did all this?"

The Truth nodded.

"It was the most amazing feat of strength," said Bandaid. She chugged ambrosia to regain her mana. "I had exhausted my mana, yet he slew the final guardian without any healing, without any help. It's a Goddamn miracle. *Gods.* I meant gods."

Mansex could only shake his head. "Truth? You're the fucking *man*, man. Chuck would be proud."

The Truth nodded again.

A light began to shimmer between the tapestries of the dragon and the lovers. They watched it blossom, invert in on itself, and collapse into a black circle: an instance, destination unknown.

"The Moon Door," said Bandaid with reverence.

PWNED

Yanker let out a long breath. "Seven seconds, people."
<Pwny Xpress> stepped through the instance and vanished.

11
Godsword

A cyclopean step pyramid filled Reid's screen. Above the loading bar, the name of the dungeon floated in a starry sky— *The First God's Tomb.* The heavens were enormous, the stars almost close enough to touch. Reid traced the constellation of the dragon with his finger.

The loading bar filled.

The portal spat the guild out onto a barren gray land-scape. Behind them, the black circle shrunk to a pinprick and vanished.

"Where are we?" Noob wondered aloud.

Dusty gray craters stretched out as far as they could see. Not a speck of life was visible anywhere. The stars above were the size of gems and painfully bright.

The Truth pointed. Up, above them, Fartherall—the game's planet—floated in the sea of stars.

"The Moon," said Noob. "Cooooool."

161

"So it is true," said Yanker. "The moon *is* a zone! Those guys from beta weren't kidding."

"Moonchart, Moon Door..." said Bandaid. "I suppose we should have put it together."

"Not to point out the obvious, but shouldn't we all be dying?" asked Noob.

"At the very least, we shouldn't be able to hear each other," said Mansex. "And we'd have frozen before we asphyxiated. I'm kind of disappointed. It's ruining my immersion."

"Really?" asked Reid. "*This* broke your suspension of disbelief? A world without toilets or permanent death, but a habitable moon, that crosses the line?"

"Would it be alright with everyone," asked Bandaid, "if I did the rest of this dungeon out of character? Just to save time?" The guild enthusiastically assented.

"Thanks," said Bandaid. "That view is fucking rad."

Noob walked over to Yanker to get a better view of the planet.

"We're on the moon," she said.

"Watch out. I hear the first step's a doozy."

They all just stood there for a moment, appreciating the CG cosmos. "You're all my good friends," said Yanker. "Thank you for being here with me." Bandaid hugged her.

"Whatever," said Mansex, throwing herself onto the hug. "Hey, you know why the moon's in space?"

"Is it because it's afraid to be on the same planet as Chuck Norris?" said Noob. Mansex glared at him. "What? That's what you were going to say, wasn't it?"

"No," said Mansex. "Not now."

The Truth tapped his wrist. *Tick tock.*

"Right," said Yanker. "Work first. Let's get going."

162

<Pwny Xpress> trekked across the lunar landscape towards the First God's tomb.

A set of stairs scaled for giants dropped down into the pyramid. At the base of the steps, a long corridor extended into a great stone maze. The walls were smooth with no visible joins, as if the maze had been carved directly into the landscape. Eddies of gray sand from the surface filled the hall, and rose in puffs from the footsteps of the clockwork automatons patrolling the corridors.

Noob toed a tiny sand dune. "This is weirdly familiar."

Bandaid looked worried. "This dungeon's *way* beyond us," she said. "Look at the monster levels. We're like twenty below the least of them."

"This place is meant to be raided, with heavy losses," said Mansex. "Fifty people might have a chance."

"Or Chuck Norris," added Bandaid.

"You're damned right."

The Truth didn't look so sure.

"Even then, a direct approach might not work," said Yanker. She was speaking in a whisper even though the patrols couldn't hear them. "A raid made it this far a month back. Found the Moonchart, took the door from the bottom of Black Chasm. They bulldozed in fifty-strong but wound up wiping 'cause their main healer got DC'd in the middle of a fight. Personally, I bet they made up that last part to save face." She looked over, and stopped. "Noob? You with us? Shit, you didn't get DC'd again, did you?"

Noob had gone rigid, staring at the sand in a corner. "She was *here*." That's where he'd seen it—the gray sand, the featureless stone architecture. *We've been in this ass-damn maze for twelve hours*. This was where she'd been when he cut the cable. He had cost her the Godsword.

No wonder she hated him. No wonder she had left.

"Who was here?" asked Yanker. "Are we missing something?"

"Alert!" yelled the game's narrator. *"Server reset in one hour!"*

"Oh, that's just wonderful," said Mansex.

"It's a Wednesday," said Bandaid. "Did we all forget it's a Wednesday?"

"Fuck!" Mansex stomped a small rage circle. "The door opens on the half-night? Seriously? There's hard, and then there's impossible!"

"I'll bet they did that intentionally," said Yanker.

"You think?"

"After last month? Absolutely. Gotta keep people playing."

"If we get booted with the reset," asked Noob, "will we still be in here when the servers come back online?"

"Do you want to wait and find out?" asked Yanker. "We've got an hour."

Great, thought Reid. "No pressure."

"Plan hasn't changed," said Yanker. She eyed the automatons. "We can't fight these fuckers, so we won't. Noob stealths to a safe spot past the patrols, Mansex teleports us to his new location. All the way to the end."

"That assumes he can find a spot without overlapping aggro," said Mansex.

"And how do we defeat whatever boss is at the end?" asked Noob.

"One thing at a time, Reid. Noob. Sorry."

"The fuck is Reid?" asked Mansex.

"Last month's raid put a map of the place on their website," said Bandaid. "I'm linking to it in chat."

"Wow," said Mansex. "When you fall off the RP wagon, you fall hard."

"It's incomplete—they didn't finish it what with getting killed and all. But it should help us for a while. Noob, go straight, then take the first left."

Noob nodded, dropped into stealth. *A month ago, I was condemning Astrid for this.* He snuck past the first of the giant clock-men.

Some time later, after a number of dead ends and wrong turns, Noob broke stealth in yet another five-way intersection. "Looks clear," he said. A second later, the guild teeped to him in a puff of pixels.

Mansex slammed her spellbook shut. "I'm almost out of mats."

"I thought you loaded before we left," Yanker said.

"I can carry 99 of a thing in my inventory. Each casting uses five, one for each of us. I've got four castings left. And I wouldn't need them if Bandy could read a fucking map."

"You know, what I really need right now is to be judged, so thank you," said Bandaid. "This map! It hasn't been right since the entrance."

"Yeah, hard to believe you couldn't trust something you found on the internet."

"It's like this is an entirely different dungeon!"

"Maybe it is," said Noob.

"We're running out of time!"

"You don't think I know that?"

"Alert! Server reset in thirty minutes!"

Mansex screamed in frustration. Bandaid cried.

"Hold it together, guys," said Yanker shakily. "We haven't come this far just to give up now. And... well, there's always next month."

In the darkness of the conference room, Reid studied the map Bandaid had linked to in guild chat. *Come on, Reid. Patterns, that's what you do, numbers and patterns. What am I missing?*

He flipped back to the game tab and pulled up the map there. "I'm looking at the map right now," he said as Noob, "last month's, and what we've scouted here, and Bandy's right. It's *not* the same dungeon. It's a chaotic, crisscrossing maze. It doesn't match."

"See?" said Bandaid. They all heard something being crumpled up and thrown. "Fuck you, map."

"Bandy," Reid asked, "What month is it?"

"March."

"In game, dumb-buns," said Mansex.

"Oh, uh... it would be... Dracinar. Month of the Dragon."

The Dragon. That rang a bell. In the month he'd been playing, it seemed like he'd been seeing a dragon everywhere, not just the glade. *But where?*

Reid pulled a marker from the drawer and drew dots on the desk, every place they'd encountered one of these five-way intersections—star-shaped intersections, it struck Reid. He connected the dots between them. The pattern was maddeningly familiar. He blinked, and when he finally saw it, he couldn't see anything else.

"It's the constellation."

The guild turned to Noob.

"The hallways, the intersections," Noob said, "they're the

Dragon! The constellation, I mean. We've been seeing it everywhere, right? The tapestries in Ord-Anmuhr, frigging right outside, right there in the sky, just staring at us. Everything related to this dungeon has had an astronomical theme, right? Moon maps and all? Why not clues in the stars?"

"Different month, different constellation. The map *was* wrong." Bandy said with relief.

"So if this month is the dragon, and the first star intersection by the entrance was his mouth, then I'm assuming his tail is the destination."

"Why not his balls?"

"Shut up, Mansex. So that means we go..." He dropped into stealth, headed down the corridor corresponding to the dragon's spine.

Yanker grinned after him and elbowed Bandaid. "*So* misnamed. Am I right?"

Seven turns and three teleports later, <Pwny Xpress> was looking through an archway at what could only be the heart of the pyramid. Hieroglyph-etched pillars ringed a cavernous room. In the center of the chamber, a column of cold light lit up a black stone sarcophagus. In an alcove beyond, a giant figure sulked on a shadowed throne.

Bandaid spotted an inscribed tablet by the entrance taller than she was. "Behold the tomb of the First God," she read, "betrayed by his children in the Godswar. Ever watchful sits His Ghost upon the Sundered Throne." She looked up. "I thought the First God was dead."

"He is," said Yanker.

"Then who's that on the throne?"

"I think we'll probably have to find out."

They padded into the chamber. Beyond the sarcophagus, in the darkened nook upon the split-backed throne sat the Ghost of the First God. Sticking out of His chest was a great sword.

"There it is," Jodie whispered. "The Godsword."

"Buried in the chest of a Level 1,000 elite," said Mansex. "Forecast tonight calls for pain."

"Right," said Yanker. "Okay. Man. He is *big*."

"And we're gonna kill him... how?" asked Bandaid. "We total half his level. This is a raid dungeon, and there's only five of us?"

"I didn't say we were gonna kill him." Yanker looked slyly at Noob. "We're just gonna distract him. While Noob picks his pocket."

Noob blinked. "I'm gonna what?"

Yanker grinned. "That's always been the plan. It's why I've groomed you the way I have," she said. "Purple Ninja Armor, maxed out on stealth and stealing. No one's ever seen what was at the back of this dungeon, so no one knows how to prepare for it... but unless they did a special tech request *just* for this encounter, then the Godsword is in his drop table, which means a rogue maxed for thieving has a *chance* of getting his sticky fingers on it."

"You *hope*," said Mansex.

"That's... kind of a crazy gamble," said Bandaid.

Yanker nodded. "I put the chances of it actually working in the ten to twenty percent range... which is *way* higher than if we'd come in here with a raid. Fifty toons, probably from different guilds, all with an equal claim to the Godsword? This is our best shot, believe me."

"Impossible," said Mansex.

Yanker nodded. "Maybe."

"Sometimes," quoted Noob, "I believe in as many as six impossible things before breakfast."

Yanker grinned.

"Well," said Mansex, "if we *do* fail, at least we're gonna fail *spectacularly*, and that's cool 'cause I don't do anything half-assed."

Noob clapped Mansex on the back, then turned to Yanker. "How do you want to do this, Captain?"

Yanker took in the pillars holding the ceiling aloft. "Okay. We'll use the terrain, these pillars here—stay out of arm's length. I'll peg him with frost arrows and glue traps. Mansex, ice-blasts. Bandy, dot him, then stay back and heal. You die, we can't rez."

"I *have* done this before, you know."

"Truth? You just keep doing your thing, man."

The Truth cracked his knuckles.

"And Noob? Stay behind him and keep spamming Pickpocket every time it refreshes. Just don't draw his aggro, 'cause I don't know that we could save you."

"I won't let you down." Reid hoped that was true.

Yanker beamed. "I hope you all realize that we're the first players to make it this far. Just let that sink in."

"Alert! Server reset in ten minutes!"

"But not for too long." She unslung her bow, nocked a pair of glue arrows. "All right, mates. Let's make histor—."

A whistle behind them.

A little baffled—but for the Ghost of the First God, the chamber appeared empty—Noob and the guild turned around.

Greef waved at them. Behind him were fifty leering members of <Something Wicked>.

"No." Yanker couldn't believe it. "How?"

"Illegal mod," said Mansex. "Has to be."

A wave from Greef, and the Wickeds attacked.

A stray arrow pierced the First God's aggro range. He looked up.

"Well, shit," said Yanker.

The First God bellowed a chamber-shaking roar and charged the raid.

The Truth leapt in front of the rampaging god, shield held high. With a single punch, the First God crushed him like an aluminum can under a sledgehammer, killing him instantly.

"Holy crapping Christ!" Mansex started casting, but Greef's net caught her and Bandaid and anchored both in place. Wickeds swarmed them. They screamed and died in tandem.

"Get the sword!" yelled Yanker. She ran from the Wickeds, straight at the First God.

The Ghost hurled a floor-splitting punch at her. Yanker darted aside, ran up his arm, and jumped to grab hold of the hilt of the sword jutting out of His chest.

Greef shrieked and pointed at Yanker. As one, the Wickeds swung their attention her way.

Yanker planted her feet on the First God's chest and heaved. "Come on!" It moved not an inch. "Come *on!* We got here first! It's *ours!*" The First God grabbed her in His fist and plucked her away. "Not fai—!"

He pulped Yanker against the floor.

"Jodie!" Noob flew to her side, but Yanker was dead.

"Reid, *move!*" Yanker's lips hadn't moved, but Jodie's message came through over guild chat. He rolled to the side.

A trunk-thick fist exploded the floor around him and splattered Yanker's body like an overripe watermelon. Noob bounced to his feet, hurled down a shadow pellet, and vanished into stealth.

Arrows and spells punched into side of the First God's head. With <Pwny Xpress> dead or vanished, it was <Something Wicked>'s turn to attack, and they turned the full force of their fifty-strong raid on the Ghost. The Ghost tore through them like a wrecking ball.

Still stealthed, Noob dodged flying dead Wickeds and wall-jumped onto the tablet by the entrance for a better view. The surviving Wickeds were attacking the First God in ranks, striking and retreating, losing at least one toon every time He counterattacked. Healers ran darting through the dead, raising what fallen they could. With thirty curses and dots over his head, the First God's health bar was slowly but steadily shrinking.

"What the fucking *no!* How can they be here?" Yanker was melting down over the GroupSpeak line. "How could they *follow* us?"

The Wickeds had eclipsed the player loss to damage ratio — the First God was shedding hit points faster than He could kill His attackers. The math was on their side, Reid realized. They were going to win. "They're gonna drop him. When can you get back here?"

"The door's closed and our healer's dead," said Yanker. "It's up to you."

"To do what? What am I supposed to do?"

"I don't *know.*" Her voice was scarcely a whisper.

A row of Wicked wizards hit the First God with a salvo of ice spells, slowing Him to a complete stop. Greef ran past a pair of necromancers — both tagged his blade with black energy charges as he passed — and backstabbed the Ghost.

The scream shook house-sized chunks of stone from the

roof and sent them exploding into the floor. Few Wickeds survived the impact, or the shrapnel. The Ghost of the First God arched, lurched, and collapsed on His back. Dead.

Greef—one of six Wickeds left alive—leapt up onto the First God's chest and grabbed the Godsword with both hands.

"Oh, no," said Yanker. It was like hearing her dream slip away. "No, no, *no, no, NO!*"

Greef heaved on the sword. It didn't budge. He screamed and tried again.

So focused was Greef on dislodging the Sword that he didn't hear the warning shouts from his own guildies. A dozen automatons summoned by the First God's dying shout stormed into the room. With mechanical precision, the remaining Wickeds—Greef included—died on whirling articulated blades.

It was suddenly eerily quiet. Everything in the room but Noob was dead. "I'm still here," he said, as much to confirm it for himself as to the guild. A trio of relieved sighs answered him.

He slid off the tablet and stealthed between patrolling automatons to the First God's body. It wasn't glowing the way a body did when there was treasure to be looted. Reid right-clicked it. A treasure window opened.

"Is it there? What is it?" asked Mansex.

"What's it look like?" Bandaid asked.

"It's empty," said Reid. It was—the treasure menu was bare. "There's nothing here."

"How can it not be there?" said Yanker. "I can *see* it in His *chest!*"

"It's not here," Noob repeated. "I don't think it ever was. The sword in the chest… I think it's part of the character model. Like a lure. Like the light on an anglerfish."

"Well then where's the Godsword?"

"I don't know!"

"Warning! Server reset in five minutes!"

Noob looked around for something, *anything*. What was the answer? What was the *puzzle*? If this wasn't the Godsword, then what was?

His eyes went from the Sword-that-wasn't-the-Godsword to the stone sarcophagus in the pillar of light. And he noticed, for the first time, that the sarcophagus was sized for a normal person—the First God wouldn't have fit in it. He stealthed over for a better look.

Twelve designs were inscribed in the lid in silver filigree, with gems inlaid at points along their outlines. One matched the constellation of the dragon. "What's in there, do you think?"

"You open that, you break stealth," said Yanker. "What the hell. Go for it."

"Yes, ma'am." Noob put his shoulder to the sarcophagus lid and pushed. It slid open with ease, and Noob became visible.

Inside was a shimmering membrane dark as jet—a black circle.

"Another instance," said Noob.

"Another one?"

The automatons buzzed in alarm and surged towards Reid, blades spinning. Noob vaulted into the casket and through the black circle.

Reid's computer screen darkened to a slate gray and pulsed as if breathing. A loading bar filled, unaccompanied by any graphic. There was no picture, no name to indicate where he was going.

He stared into the gray of the screen. His senior year, the

night after he'd lost his virginity to Astrid, he had driven out to Owen Beach—a tiny stretch of stony shore in Point Defiance his grandparents had liked to take him to as a child.

It had been 2:00am when he snuck into the park, walking down into the grass bowl from a street that ran perpendicular to the closed gate. It had been foggy that night, so foggy that he couldn't see the massive sentinel trees around the duck ponds until he could nearly touch them. By memory more than sight, he had stumbled his way through the park's interior roads and found the fenced, wooded cliff that ran around the rim of the park.

By the time he had arrived at the beach, the fog had grown so thick that the only lights he could see were from the ferry dock on Vashon Island. Then the fog had thickened and swallowed those, too, and the gray of the clouds blended in with the gray of the water until he couldn't tell where sky ended and sea began. It was a vast expanse of gray nothing, a blank canvas. He had reached the end of the world.

Reid had brought Astrid to Owen Beach at night as often as she'd come. But the sky was never was as foggy as it had been that first night.

The first time, they'd brought vodka in a Nalgene, and the water had been glassy enough for them to see the bioluminescent *noctiluca* plankton in the Sound. They had spent hours running cold-numbed fingers through the water, watching the trail of tiny flashes flit across the surface.

The second night, the sky had opened up. They'd gotten lost in the rain, and wound up in the rose tunnel near the pagoda. It was the second time they made love.

The third night, they had decided to try a different trail, and found themselves in a garden abutting a concrete walkway

that ran from Owen Beach back to the marina. They had cuddled in a tree shaped like a hand, with palm pointing to the sky,
and from there watched the sun rise. Astrid had come back
with pneumonia, and after that, she'd never snuck into Point
Defiance at night with Reid again.

The last time Reid had snuck into the park himself had
been three years ago, after his grandfather's funeral. He hadn't
planned to go—the day had drained him enough—but as he
was undoing his tie, he caught a glimpse of the heavy fog rolling towards Commencement Bay. He had gotten to the park
as fast as he could through the wind and the rain, running the
entire way, ruining his suit.

He had reached the beach, but it was too windy: the fog
kept rolling, never quite thick enough to blot out the world on
the night he most needed the world blotted out. *Sorry kid*, the
universe seemed to be saying. *You get what you need once. After
that, you're on your own.* He hadn't been back since.

"Where are you?" It was Yanker's voice. Jodie's. "Are you
still alive?"

"I don't know," Reid heard himself saying. In his mind, he
was still on the beach, staring at the end of the world.

The loading bar filled, and the gray fog parted.

Noob found himself standing in a vast, empty space.

"Everything's dark," he told the guild. "Wait. There's something there." Far ahead, something shimmered. He ran toward
it.

Ahead, in a pillar of light, lay a kind-faced old man on a
patch of grassy earth. He looked like the First God, but man-
sized, and frail—human. Tendrils of grass and flowers had
grown over and around him and twined through his hair. A

sword—human-sized and real—rose from the First God's chest, just above where his hands were folded.

Reid moused over the sword. It lit up.

"It's here," Reid said. "We found it."

Cheers erupted over his headset, caws of joy and relief. Reid beamed.

"Wait for us!" said Yanker. "Wherever you are, we're gonna rez and see if we can teleport to you."

Reid's eyes went to the picture of Astrid in the frame of his screen. His smile died, and he ground his eyes shut. *Remember the beach.* "Guys. This whole thing has been... way more fun than I expected."

We went skinny dipping in the flashing water. We cuddled afterwards to chase the cold away.

"You're all great people. Even Mansex."

"You sound like you're about to fire us or something," said Yanker. The others chuckled. Reid didn't chuckle back, and when they heard that, they fell silent.

Peel away all the bullshit, that's what's real.

"It's my only way to get her back. I have to do this."

It was very quiet on the other end of the line. "Noob?" Yanker said. "You're kind of freaking me out."

"I'm sorry."

"What, you... *ninja!*" yelled Mansex.

The line erupted in nervous laughter and pleas, insistence that he was just kidding, that he'd better hurry up and snag the damn thing and please dear God make some sort of sound so I know you're not doing what you're pretending you're going to do.

"Noob?" Jodie's voice cut through the din. "Please."

"Jodie, I'm sorry."

"Don't do this! *Reid?*"

"She's all I get."

Reid yanked off his headset. The guild's muffled protests drifted up from the earpiece on the floor.

His hand quivering, Reid opened the "Group Options" tab on the game menu, selected *Leave Group.* The voices abruptly cut out.

Reid warily lifted the headset, said "Hello?" into the mic. There was no reply.

This is the right thing. He rubbed tears out of his eyes. *I don't owe them anything. I don't even* know *them, not really—I only just heard their voices today. They were gonna use me. They needed the Moonchart, remember? I just beat them to it, that's all. It's not like you'll have to meet them face to face, especially not Jodie—Yanker— living on the other side of the ocean.*

Easier to be the one who leaves. He wondered if he'd ever believe any of it.

A message popped up on screen: *"Warning! Server reset in one minute!"*

"Let's get this over with." He moused over the Godsword icon and clicked.

With one smooth motion, Noob withdrew the Godsword from the First God's chest.

Another message popped up: *This item begins a quest.*

Reid blinked. *"Begins* a quest?" He accepted the quest and read the requirements:

Speak with the First God.

The First God's eyes opened. He sat up and regarded Reid. A treasure chest icon appeared above his head. Reid clicked.

The First God spoke. "In removing the Godsword, you have freed me from a fate most arduous. For many years, I have awaited a hero of your promise."

Reid snorted. "Hero."

"Your worth has been proven. A true master player you are. There is but one task left for you to accomplish. And that... is to *party!*"

Mariachi music erupted from nowhere, and confetti and balloons showered down. Dancing animated toons of what could only be the design team (judging by the prevalence of ponytails and Hawaiian shirts) faded in behind the First God. They blew noisemakers and a disco ball dropped into view.

"Congratulations!" continued the First God. "You'll be the Player Guest of Honor at the next HowdyCon, and attend *all* the events at the con with the designers as an honorary member of the Design Team! That includes a backstage pass, your portrait on the Wall of Heroes at Boy Howdy, and a seat at the HowdyCon banquet table with the game's creators, where you'll get to tell us what you love the most about *Fartherall Online!*"

The First God sat up and donned a pair of sunglasses. "I guarantee it. After all, you've got this—" He did the snapguns with his fingers. "God's word."

Ah, Reid thought distantly. *It* was *God's word after all*.

The First God blew a party horn in Noob's face.

A meeting. It hit Reid like a bomb in the gut. The Godsword was a meeting. An in with Boy Howdy.

"Server reset in five... four..."

"Oh, Yanker."

"Three... two..."

"Jodie."

The world went white, and then went away.

PWNED

12
Ninja

TIP: Be courteous while in a group, and you'll be invited back!

Once Reid found the line item where Engelbrook-Meyer had been hiding its money, the work fell like a line of dominoes. He went through each section summary—that part of the dream had been accurate, at least—and flagged the recurring incongruity on each page.

Official company policy was to never call tax fraud what it was, but to treat each and every meticulously planned infraction as if it had been an accident. "Consider reviewing," he penned into the margins by each disparity. "Blatant felony" would have been more accurate, and probably would have gotten him fired. Not that he particularly cared at the moment.

Reid finished around 4:30am. Somewhere along the line, he realized, he'd become good at his job—helping his company help multinationals avoid paying their taxes. *This is my life,* he thought. *This was what I've put my youth into—helping rich people cheat on their taxes. I've gotten very good at cheating.*

When 7:30 rolled around, Habermann found Reid nibbling on a packaged muffin with his feet on the conference room table. Habermann sighed and looked at the ceiling. "Reid, Reid, Reid…" He must have assumed he hadn't finished. "What does the manual say about deadlines?"

Reid tossed him the file folder. "They hid it in office supplies," he said. "Seems Engelbrook, or maybe it was Meyer, accidentally spent $85 million more on paperclips than they meant to. I'm guessing they should've spent that money on shredders."

Habermann gave the folder a cursory review. "You finished."

"Hence the Victory Muffin."

"Very good, Reid. I'm very pleased with your work. The Board will be, too."

"Thumbs up to board." He raised his thumb. Habermann returned the gesture, and returned to his office.

Reid glanced back at the clock. The game would be back online in ninety minutes. Ninety minutes, and he'd have Astrid's information.

The Victory Muffin tasted like ashes.

The coffee maker sputtered and coughed phlegmatically. I wasn't built for the abuse Reid had been putting it through.

Reid splashed water on his face from the sink. He considered washing his hair under the faucet with dish soap, but opted instead to fill the basin and submerge his head. For a cold, quiet moment, the world went away.

"Did you hear? Someone found the Godsword."

"No kidding?"

Dimly, Reid recognized their voices. Two of the unpaid interns—the spiky-haired guy with the spray tan, and the skinny kid with the contacts who was blinking all the time. The company wasn't planning to hire either of them.

"Yeah, bulletin went out this morning over realm chat," said Blinky. "And the guy who got it? Word is he pulled a total ninja, stabbed his group in the back."

"Damn," said Spraytan. "What a douchey thing to do."

"No doubt. Total jerk."

"That's the end of that guild."

They trailed off when they noticed Reid staring at them, water streaming from his face. Eventually, Blinky asked "Are you okay, Mr. Underwood?"

"My head is wet."

"Do you want some paper towels?"

"We're out."

"I could get you some from the men's room," said Spraytan.

"Yes, thank you."

After toweling off, Reid poured his coffee and retreated to the conference room. Lodge found him there packing folders into file boxes.

"Hey," he said. "Did you finish?"

"Yep."

"With the project, or the sword quest?"

"Both."

"Well. I suppose congratulations are in order." Reid kept packing. "So... does Astrid come home today?"

Reid glared at him until Lodge retreated. "I hope so," Reid said, after he'd gone. *Do I hope so? I hope I hope so.*

His watch alarm beeped. The game was back online. Reid closed the conference room door and angled his monitor away from the wall of windows facing into the office. *Just a little bit longer, and I'll be done. I'll finally be done.*

＊ ＊ ＊

Marrowstone City thrummed. Noob couldn't see the street ahead of him through the throng of players. It was worse than a subway car at rush hour. Worse than trying to walk the exhibit hall floor at Comic Con. Noob could barely move.

The crowd was thickest outside the town hall. It looked for the world like the whole continent had turned out. Maybe it had. The crowd went clear out the door, across the field and into Inkwood.

The door to town hall creaked open. The Town Crier, ringing his bell. "Hear ye, hear ye! The spirit of the First God has been laid to rest! The Godsword has been retrieved!"

A tsunami of thwarted entitlement hit the town. Hundreds of level-capped characters broke down and cried. Others vented their frustration by stabbing each other—a meteor shower of dueling stones slammed into the ground. If the game had police cars, the crowd would have overturned them and set them on fire. The town hall was already in flames.

Noob dropped into stealth and maneuvered through the carnage and fire. He found the Admin at the back of his alley, the bright yellow "A" a lighthouse bulb above his head.

The Admin scoffed when Noob unstealthed in front of him. "Oh, great. It's you. Before you ask, the answer's no. The Godsword was the only thing I was interested in, and now that it's gone, I'm not risking my job for you."

"I got it."

"Right. You're the über-leet dude with the über-leet skills who did what no player in three years managed to."

Reid showed him the Godsword via a trade window. Speechless, the Admin reached for it.

Noob closed the menu. "Oh, no, no, *no*," he chided. "This

was a quid pro quo, remember?"

"Holy crap." The Admin kept looking where the menu had been, as if he could will it back into existence. "It was you? I mean, *you*?"

Noob nodded.

The Admin cheered and burst into dance. "No way! Man! I can't believe you did it! I mean *you*, of all people! My God! Ninja for the win, am I right? Ha! You totally ninja'd Pwny Xpress! Oh! I love it. Fuck those guys."

"That's my guild you're talking about."

"Not for much longer, I'm guessing. So come on, who are you? Who's your main? You seriously had me going with this 'Noob' character. Was that just style points, then? Come on, you can tell me. Who is it who pulled one over on that Yanker cunt and the freak team?"

"Watch it, guy."

"Let's see, you'd have had to be off for like the last whole month or so, so…"

"Can we just get this over with, please? I'm at work."

"Sure, boss! Keep your secret. I'll find you online when you brag about this. Okay, let's knock this out. Gimme your girl's name, and I'll give you her account info. Address, email, phone number. Skype ID. Hell, I'll give you her fucking credit card. Everything!"

"You watch your mouth about Pwny Xpress. They're good people."

"Hey, sure thing, man. Don't mean to get you steamed."

"We did it with five, okay? The Godsword dungeon, the run to and through the door, with *five*. That was a dungeon fifty couldn't handle."

"Yes, you're amazing. By your holy foot are all asses kicked.

Let's make the trade."

"They taught me how to play. Trained me to be one of them. My guild's been looking for that sword for *months.*"

"So's mine," said the Admin. "So's everyone's. It's an epic quest. Your girl's name: what is it?"

"I betrayed them for it." Reid said it out loud as he typed. It sucked the breath from his chest to say it. He felt like he was about to start hyperventilating.

"Yes, your balls are big, brass, and shiny, and lesser men shall shine them and thank you for the honor. Look, I can't help you get your girlfriend if you don't give me her damn name."

We're almost done, Reid thought. *Come on, nearly there.* He forced his attention back to the game.

Noob pulled up the treasure window with the Godsword in it. "It's Astrid. Astrid Wheeler."

"Fuck. Me. So that means—Oh, my God."

Noob didn't hear him. He was too busy staring at the Godsword. In the worldwide player base, he alone knew what it really was. Not a weapon, not a trophy, but a meeting with the gods. Every player's dream. Especially that of the woman who'd been willing to help him in the first place.

Reid closed the treasure window. "I'm sorry. Deal's off."

"Whoa," said the Admin. "Hey. Hold on, now."

"Forget it. I don't want it." He really didn't.

"I've got her information right here!"

"Sorry. I've changed my mind." Noob strode out of the alley.

The city square was an inferno from hell. NPC guards had formed a bucket brigade by the well. A few lowbies were help-ing them heave buckets onto the fire, and were earning enough XP doing so to level over and over in alternating bursts of light.

The sight made Noob grin and hurt—he'd leveled that fast once, with Jodie leading the way.

The Admin caught up Noob and slipped in front of Noob— much like he'd done with Jodie when she'd first left him for the woods. *Jodie. I need to find Jodie.*

"You can't just go! We had a deal!" the Admin yelled. "Don't you want Astrid to come home?"

Reid didn't know anymore. "I *can't* give it to you. It belongs to someone else."

The Admin bellowed enraged gibberish. Noob expected him to start stabbing a building and setting townsfolk on fire. It seemed to be the trend. "We had a deal," the Admin cried. "Here, I'll send you the info anyway."

"You don't need to do that."

"I trust you'll do the right thing and give me the sword."

"Trust? I'm a freaking ninja, remember?"

"Seriously, *please*. Just... give me your password, and I'll email you the info. Okay? Amin's honor." The Admin gave him the three finger salute.

"I still won't give it to you."

"Whatever. I'll find it on my own," said the Admin. "Karma's coming your way." He sat and vanished.

Noob set off through the inferno towards the Roaring Hearth Inn. A salvo of distraught players hurled themselves off of the cathedral and splattered to death behind him. Moments later, they rezzed, only to run back up and throw themselves off again.

They'd planned to meet here after the quest, after they'd found the Godsword. That was before they'd forgotten about the server reset. And before he'd stolen the thing. Noob sat in his chair by the fire and wondered if they'd show.

"Didn't expect to see you here."

Jodie's voice in his ear. Noob jumped up and turned. She was standing at the entrance with the rest of the guild. They were all keeping their distance, all scowling.

"Your girl," said Jodie. "I hope she's worth it. You're out of the guild."

"That's fair."

Trumpets lamented. The <Pwny Xpress> logo vanished from Noob's tabard, leaving it a flat slate gray. <Pwny Xpress> disappeared from under his name, leaving him as he'd started—just another Noob. He looked up at his former guildmates. "Jodie, I'm sorry."

"You don't get to call me that. Nobody gets to call me that."

Bandaid laid a hand on Yanker's shoulder. "We don't have to do this here."

"I want you out the game. Like you promised, remember? 'Help me with this one thing and you'll never see me again.' I'm calling that in."

"Okay." *You never* have *seen me.* "I just have something to give you first."

"I don't want anything from you."

"You'll want this. You earned it."

He opened a trade window and made it public in the common room—the Godsword, visible to everyone. Jodie caught her breath.

The guild stared. Incredulous mutters filled the chat channel: my god, there it is, it's on our server, the Godsword's in the inn, Roaring Hearth not Drunkfucker's.

"I thought you…" Jodie trailed off. Reid couldn't tell what was winning the war for her voice: delight, anger, fear.

Something he couldn't place. "I thought you needed that."

"Yeah, well. What we think we need... I'll find some other way."

"You're serious?" Hope. That's what it was.

"It's yours," said Reid. "And I'll still leave the game. If that's what you want."

Bandaid scoffed. "Oh, you idiot."

"What I *want?*" said Yanker. "Seriously, mate. How thick are—?"

The screen froze.

The game kicked Reid to the login screen, where a message read: *You have been disconnected.*

"Oh, come *on!*" Reid tried logging back in. Nothing happened. He checked his account name, entered the password again.

Another message popped up: *Someone else has logged in to that account.*

Reid paled. "Oh, no. Oh, no no no no no."

A crowd had gathered around Noob's open trade window, gaping at the Godsword. Some reached for it, but the only one who could touch it was the one it had been opened for—Yanker. Mansex elbowed her, and she reached for the blade.

The window abruptly closed. Yanker blinked at Noob. "Don't tell me you're changing your mind again."

Noob smirked. He skipped to the mailbox in the corner of the inn and dropped the Godsword in. It vanished to a collective gasp from the crowd.

"Did you..." Yanker's shoulders drooped. "Did you just mail it to me?"

Noob shook his head. Then he saluted the guild and gave Yanker the middle finger.

"You fucking wanker!" Yanker erupted. "Ninja bastard! What's *wrong* with you?"

She fell silent as the name above Noob's head switched from blue to red. He'd entered PVP mode.

"Hear ye, hear ye!" The Town Crier stepped into the inn, mechanically clanging his bell. "The spirit of the First God has been laid to rest!"

Noob backstabbed the Crier. He squealed, pitched forward, and landed dead on his bell.

The assembled players gaped at Noob. He vanished into stealth.

Reid's computer had just rebooted from a restart. He tried logging in again and got the same message: *Someone else is logged in to that account.*

"No!" He smacked his computer. "It's not me!"

Bandaid shrieked and died, Noob's blade in her back. The action broke his stealth. Before anyone could act, Noob leapt onto Mansex and dragged her to the ground with a garotte.

Mansex got off a couple of fireballs that set the ceiling on fire before Noob hurled the still gurgling mage into the fireplace. She ignited with a mighty whoosh.

Yanker unslung her bow, drew. Noob vanished.

Behind Yanker, a lowbie screamed, cut in half. Noob didn't reappear—the lowbie had been too low-level to break his stealth. Another onlooker's throat opened ear to ear.

Yanker drew a glitter-tipped arrow and fired it into the

ceiling. A shower of sparkles coated everything in the room with golden dust—including the translucent shape now hurtling straight for her. She didn't have time to drop her bow before Noob stabbed her in the heart.

"Fucking *come. On.*" Boy Howdy customer service was busy, and Reid was running out of carpet to pace.

An email landed in Reid's inbox. Not his work email, but in the personal account he kept minimized on his desktop. It was from a Boy Howdy account, something about account security. "Oh, thank God."

Reid threw himself in the chair, opened it. He skimmed down a page of boilerplate blah blah to a link that said "Restore Account" and clicked it.

The computer froze. He clicked the mouse a couple times, but couldn't move the cursor. "What *now?*"

A browser tab opened to a website he didn't recognize. Then he did, and ice stabbed his spine. It was the <Something Wicked> guild forums.

Specifically, it was a new discussion topic called "For Noob." There was a single post in it. That post read: *God, you're fucking dumb.*

That's when Reid noticed a confirmation prompt on his screen: *"Are you sure you want to delete all files on Drive C?"*

Reid clicked *no.* Or tried to. The cursor wasn't moving for him. But it *was* moving—towards *yes.*

"Oh, shit." Someone had taken remote control of his desktop. Reid dove under the computer and yanked the plug.

But not fast enough. When he'd logged back in, his work—and the Englebrook-Meyer return—were gone.

Reid didn't quite remember hurling the computer into the

wall. But he'd never forget the look of shock on Habermann's face, or the surprised gaggle of glowering old guys his boss had just led into the break room.

"Ah," said Habermann. He seemed to deflate. "This..." He opened and closed his mouth a few times before gesturing feebly to Reid. "This is the talented young man I was telling you about who... singlehandedly managed... the Englebrook-Meyer...." He trailed off. Habermann swallowed. "Say hello to the Board, Reid."

The cold-faced men did not seem impressed. And that was before one of the Board members noticed Reid's copy of *Fartherall Online.*

A half hour later, the six unpaid interns were polishing their resumes as Reid carried a box of belongings into the parking lot.

13
Antagonist

TIP: If you're having trouble completing a quest,
you might be too low level.
Try again when you have more experience!

Reid fell asleep on the sofa next to his box of office trinkets. He dreamed the mouse magnets had come to life and were making out on the floor. He shouted at them to be quiet and not rub his face in it, but the boy mouse just shot him an annoyed look and said "Hey, asshole, I know what I want," before resuming mousey smooches.

A knock woke him up. Zombie-eyed, he trudged to the door and yanked it open.

It was Astrid. She had her keys in her hand as if she hadn't decided whether to bolt or not. "Hey," she said. "I heard what happened. You okay?"

"Hey," he said, for the purpose of having something to say. "I'm, uh... not great." He ground his palms into his eyes and rubbed. She was still there afterward. "Sorry. It's just, I've kinda hallucinated something very similar to this."

"What?"

"What are you doing here, Astrid?"

"I wanted to check on you."

"Sorry, no, I... How are you?"

She smiled. "Good," she said. "Really good, actually." She looked it. She had a light in her eyes he hadn't seen for a while. A couple years at least.

"Good," he repeated. "That's good, yeah. And, uh… *where* have you—?"

"Yes! Bellingham. Should have said." She nodded a few times. "I've been staying at Stacy's. She had a roommate move out last semester so there was a couch to crash on."

"Stacey…" He couldn't quite place the name.

"From TCC, before I… well." She had dropped out, a couple months after she'd started playing.

"Stacey. I think I remember her"

"She's been studying for her masters in hospitality." The smile came back. "At Western."

"Cool," said Reid.

Astrid still hadn't come in. Reid stepped out of the doorframe, gestured into the apartment, in case she was waiting for permission. She didn't move. She kind of flinched, actually.

"I'm sorry about the sword," she blurted.

"What?"

"Greef. He was bragging about it. In guild chat, where everyone could hear it."

"… What?"

"Can I come in?"

"Of course. You live here." He waved her in and sat on the couch. She noticed the box of his office stuff, and her eyes widened.

"Oh, shit. He *did* get you fired."

"No. Just unpaid leave."

Habermann had only taken him aside for a few minutes, but it had felt like hours. The boss he'd always assumed hated him was blinking back tears when he stammered how he'd let Reid down, how he should have found some way to let him know about the test. But that's how the Board looked for leadership candidates: give an impossible task, an unfair one, and see how they'd act. Do they complain? Cheat? Quit? He had been bringing the Board in to show Reid off when snapped and launched his computer into the wall. He'd chucked any chance of advancement with it. All the Board had seen was a tantrum from a brat playing video games at work.

His boss had saved his job, but it would be another year or two until Habermann could retire now. Another year or two to find another successor. Reid would have been less ashamed if Habermann had fired him outright.

"Did you know," he asked Astrid, "that Habermann liked me? Like, was grooming me for a promotion?"

She blinked. "Yes. Not about the promotion thing—that's *awesome*—but... He *adored* you. You were like... mini-him. You *never* picked up on that?"

Reid looked at the floor. "I'm pretty bad at picking up what's going on."

Astrid grunted.

"So you're a Wicked?"

She sighed, covered her face with a hand. "I'm their main healer. I *started* that damn guild."

Reed remembered the figure in the woods, back on the first day. *R-something.* "You were in the woods when Greef jumped Yanker."

"Yeah, that was... God." She shook her head. "I don't

even… He's such an asshole. I don't know if he thinks that shit actually impresses me, or if he's just trying to rub my nose in it."

"What?"

"It used to be *my* guild," she said. "But then I did what you do when you want to run raids—I recruited. And after I went dead in the middle of the Godsword run, he convinced them I wasn't competent enough to run the guild. That night in the woods? I was trying to get *away* from him, but he insisted on following me, on *escorting* me. *For my own protection.* Jesus, dude, I can auto heal and stone bubble, I don't need your help."

"He killed Yanker."

"Yeah. I didn't know you were the noob he was camping. I can't *stand* that fucker."

"Then why—"

"Because it's *my guild.*" Her eyes were burning. "Sorry. You wouldn't understand."

Guilt stabbed him over and over. He wondered what <Pwny Xpress> was up to. "I'm sorry."

She waved that away. "Wickeds… they're mostly okay, really. I mean yeah, we're at war, but still… he's fucking *guild-master* now. I've only been sticking around to get him voted out, but he convinced everyone we were gonna find the Godsword, and then we *did.*"

"*We* did," said Reid. "He stole it from me."

"Yeah," she said. "He's an admin. It's how he knows where to find all those fucking mods, and of course everyone just *goes along with it*, since they're playing to win."

She stopped and ran a hand through her hair. "He tried to *give* it to me," she said. "In public. He's always doing that shit. Offers me the best loot, the rarest drops, *over guild chat* so everyone can fucking hear, and then gets pissy when I *repeat* that I'm

not. Interested. Like he wants me to fucking owe him something."
She shook her head in disgust. "We *never* should have moved
to GuildSpeak. I could've kept pretending I was a guy. Fuck."

Reid was reeling. "I had no idea."

"Yeah, well…" She crossed her arms, leaned against the
bookshelf.

"I thought you *liked* the game."

"I *love* it. There's just a heavy of infusion of assholes in
there."

"You spent more time in there than here."

She clenched her jaw. "It felt *safe* to say things there, you
know? To people you never have to meet. To vent. About stuff.
About you."

"I… yeah."

"He said he was *saving* me from my asshole stalker ex." She
couldn't look at him. "I didn't even know you were playing."

"We were chatting, though," said Reid. "Night of the
Godsword, you and me. I told you how to get past the Titans."

"Yeah. I thought maybe if I could get them to the
Godsword—fuck."

"What?"

"Yeah."

Reid sighed. "Could we talk about something happy?"

She nodded. "Okay. Like what?"

"Well…" She'd come home. He should be ecstatic. "Hey!
You're back. That's good, right?"

She didn't change expression.

Something dawned on Reid. "You're not, though. Are you?"

She shook her head.

"I've been sitting in on some classes. With Stacey. They're
really… I'm…" She turned her head, but she couldn't hide the

smile. "I enrolled. I start this fall. I'm going back to school."

"Wow. That's great. For hospitality?" She nodded. "Going for your extreme B&B?"

"Maybe?" she said. "I don't know. But it feels right. And if I don't have to worry about rent for this place, I can afford classes *and* the room at Stacey's. Dad can't refuse to pay for anything that isn't real estate if *I'm* paying for the whole fucking thing." She beamed.

Reid realized she hadn't brought any bags with her. "You're not coming back."

She flushed. "I haven't really been here for a while."

Reid nodded. He was relieved that he felt glad for her. That would help him through the crying later. "If that's what you want to be doing, then why're you always playing?"

"To get jerkface voted out."

"No," said Reid. "I mean... before. Here."

Her face went taut. "It was easier than dealing with you."

Reid grunted. He didn't think he could feel any sicker. "So why'd you stay with me?"

"Because," she said quietly, "you were my Boo-Bear." *Were.* "You needed me. After your grandparents... You just *stopped.* You were just this lump of sadness. Nothing made you happy, nothing was good enough. I couldn't take care of you *and* me. I fucking *stopped going to school* because it was too much. And after a while I was like 'I need to get out of here, but I can't,' and the game was like a compromise. And you hated it, which made it better, so..." She trailed off.

"I get it," said Reid. "I didn't just cut the cord. I cut your lifeline."

Her eyes were misting. "I *tried* to make it work," she said. "God damn it." She *hated* crying. "It's just, I *couldn't,* okay? And

I couldn't *say* anything because you think you'll *die* if you're alone, and I *can't have* that shit on me."

You've got a good woman there, Frank had told him. *You hold on to her.* His wife had died, and then so had he. Without his mom, Reid's dad might as well have been dead. *This shit got imprinted deep,* thought Reid.

Astrid dug the tears out of her eyes and wiped her hands on her shirt. "Okay? I'm sorry."

Reid was crying too. "I..." He didn't even know where to start. "I'm sorry I was holding you back. I should have known I was, but I was just... I had no idea I was the bad guy."

"You're not the bad guy," she said. "Not really. Just a noob. Everyone sucks at first."

Reid blurted a laugh. "I'm a noob at a lot, I guess."

She grinned her lopsided grin. "Hey, so... if it's cool, I'm gonna bring a truck down this weekend and get the rest of my stuff."

"Yeah, of course."

"If you need any help with... whatever, just—" He nodded. "Okay." She clapped once, let out a long breath. "Starting to feel awkward now."

"Yeah. To make that worse, could I have my grand-mother's... ?"

"Jesus! Yes, of course." She dug for the ring in her pocket, which made it a little easier to accept—Reid couldn't imagine how much it would've hurt to learn she'd still been wearing it.

Reid didn't even try to sleep that night. He stood on the apartment balcony and watched the cars pass until the streets were empty. He'd always been afraid of being alone. Now that he undeniably was, he found it kind of comforting. *No one to disappoint but myself.*

The fog crept in sometime after midnight. It was slow and thick, like a rolling pea soup, and Reid followed it to Point Defiance. He hiked past the sentinel trees by memory, past the rose garden where he and Astrid had made love, down to the garden at the base of the cliff where the bioluminescent plankton had put on their show. The fog swallowed starlight and fog light and painted the world a blank gray again.

He stood at the end the world, looked out on a blank gray canvas, and thought *Well, this is some maudlin bullshit.* It let him laugh at himself.

Reid went home and slept better than he had in years.

14
Endgame

TIP: Use of illegal modifications is prohibited.
Violators are subject to bans and having their accounts deleted.

The sunset painted Mirror Lake a vibrant orange and pink. A bobber splashed into the water and sent sorbet ripples along the surface.

The Truth reeled his fishing line back to the shallows. On shore, Bandaid sat in meditation and tried to ignore Mansex's erotic dancing in her face. "Stop dancing, whore."

"Die in a fire, prude."

A level-capped toon ran up to the trio and jumped up and down for their attention. He was a guildless human rogue named Boon.

"Hey," he said in Reid's voice. "It's me. I still had your GroupSpeak line."

Mansex stopped dancing. She and Bandaid glared. The Truth just turned back to his fishing.

"Boon, huh?" said Mansex. "Surprised that name wasn't taken."

"It was. I paid some Fillipino kid $200 for the name."

"You had another 100?" asked Bandaid.

Boon shook his head. "Boy Howdy deleted my main after Greef took him for a spin. Dude downloaded an illegal mod that let him go PVP against his own faction, and that was enough for a death sentence, so…" he shrugged.

"So this is an alt?" asked Mansex. "Doesn't it take like 500 hours of gameplay to hit 100? Or did you find another guild to fuck over?"

"I did it solo," said Reid. He was glad they couldn't smell him, or see the compost heap his apartment had become

Bandaid whispered something to Mansex. The two got up and left without a glance Boon's way.

"It's okay that you hate me," Boon said on the GroupSpeak line. "That's entirely justified. But it's not too late—I know how to fix things. About the sword, I mean. We can still get the Godsword back if we hurry." They kept walking.

"They can't hear you." The voice was one Reid hadn't heard before, strong and smooth, supple as a pair of weathered leather gloves.

Boon wasn't sure who'd spoken. The voice was teasingly familiar. "They can't?"

"They've switched lines. It's the only reason I'm talking to you now."

The only nearby player tranquilly cast his line into the lake. *No, it couldn't be.* "The Truth? Is that you?"

The Truth nodded.

"All that time?" said Boon. "All that time, you were listening? Hearing every conversation, every word?"

"Words are distractions," said The Truth, "Man's attempt to encapsulate the ineffable. People hide behind them, even past the point where what they want is patently clear. Actions are where to look for truth and character—they're one and the same. As it was when you betrayed us."

Reid wasn't going to argue. "I don't have any excuses. I screwed you. All of you, and I'm sorry. I... didn't have my head on right, not that that matters."

"What has been done cannot be undone. The past is gone, lost to us all. The future is unwritten and unknowable, a blank canvas."

Ha, thought Reid.

"If you want change," said The Truth, "take action in the present. Only the now is within your grasp."

"That's..." That was very much like what his grandmother would have said. "Thank you."

The Truth turned back to his fishing.

"Okay," said Reid. "Here's what I came to say. Please just hear me out, and please pass this on to Yanker if I can't find her today." *I always seem to be looking for a woman in this game.* "We've still got a chance to get the Godsword back."

The Truth cocked an ear.

"Greef doesn't know how to use the Godsword. He wasn't there when the First God spoke, so he didn't get the directions *or* the quest he needs to redeem the reward. The quest giver he'd have to turn the Sword in to is still there—I've checked— and I'm guessing that means he's got to go *back* to the moon to get the quest, right? But the only way back is through another Moongate, and I know where the next one is going to be."

When he hadn't been leveling Boon, Reid had spent the month combing forums and rumor sites. He joined pick-up groups for dungeon raids and helped other players find the clues, and took notes instead of his share of the loot. He'd pieced together where and when the next gate would open along the way.

"And that's where Something Wicked will be," he finished, "camping the dungeon until the Moongate opens. That's where we hit them and take back the Sword."

"And where's that?" It was Bandaid who asked. Boon turned to see her and Mansex standing atop the hill by the lake. They must have started listening in again.

"Our backyard," he told them, "the Moonhollow Ruins, straight through there." Boon pointed towards Inkwood, the zone Yanker warned a Level 1 Noob to steer clear of ages ago. "What do you say? Are you in?"

"Mm." Bandaid pursed her lips, regarded Mansex. "I'm in if Yanker is."

"That's good enough for me. Where *is* Yanker?"

Bandaid and Mansex looked at one another. "We don't know," said Mansex. "Haven't seen her since you turned coat. So hooray, we don't have a ranger. Or a leader. Don't tell her I said that, okay?"

"She hasn't been answering messages or guild chat," said Bandaid. "I don't know if she's even playing any more."

Boon grunted. "If she is, I think I know where."

Reid found Yanker watching the dragon from the edge of the glen, and sat Boon down beside her. "I figured you'd be here."

She didn't look at him. "Thought you were leaving the game."

"I did."

"So what brought you back?"

Boon rubbed his hands. "I'm gonna assume you've been listening in." She didn't contradict him. "Tonight's the night the new Moongate opens. The Wickeds have already gone into the dungeon by now."

"And you know that how?"

"They burned down the monastery on their way in. It's kind of their thing. Also, I've got someone on the inside. If we hurry, we can still catch Greef before the Moon Door opens. It's not too late to get the Godsword back."

She scoffed. "I don't really care about that any more."

"You should."

"Oh, and why's that?"

"Because it's not a weapon. It's not a trinket, not an artifact, not anything you can equip."

"Whoop-de-shit."

"It's an invitation." She blinked and turned to look at him. "A Guest of Honor invitation to the next HowdyCon."

"Is that all?"

"No. The Godsword's literally a seat at the table with the creators of the game. A two-hour window to talk *Fartherall Online* with the people who are making it. It's your chance — share your philosophy, impress them, and get yourself hired. They'll listen to you — you're the person who got to the Godsword *first*, with a five-person team. They'll listen. And even if they don't, other companies will be there. It's a foot in the door. No bullshit."

Her eyes were huge.

"But," he continued, "if the Wickeds get to the Moon and Greef carries that sword into the First God's casket, that's it — he'll know where to turn in the sword, and the Wickeds will get the seat at the table."

"What about your girl? The one you needed the sword for."

"Turned out she hadn't been my girl for a long time."

"Sorry."

"It's for the best. So—we get the Sword from the Wickeds before they get to the First God's Tomb, you've got a shot at your dream job. A shot—it's only a meeting; you've got to do the rest. And you'll never have to see me again. I mean it this time."

Boon stood up, smoothed his garments. "If you'd like to help, we'll be in the Moonhollow. Be careful in Inkwood. It's absolute death in there." He strode back up the path.

Yanker watched him go, and went back to watching the dragon.

<Pwny Xpress> clustered around the entrance to the Moonhollow dungeon.

"You're sure they're here?" asked Bandaid. There were no other guilds around, no one killing each other to be first through the portals. "It's dead out here."

"No raids killing each other," said Mansex. "I kinda miss that."

"And no extra security," said Bandaid. "No titans, golems or whatever."

"As far as the player base knows, the Godsword's claimed and gone," said Boon. "And I'm guessing Boy Howdy isn't going out of its way to advertise that it *isn't*."

"True dat," mused Mansex.

"Even the people finding the Moonchart clues think they're leftovers from drop tables that haven't been updated."

"Maybe I'm missing something," said Bandaid, "but how are we even supposed to follow them in? We'll get our own instance of the dungeon and be in a completely separate space."

"Normally, yes," said Boon, "but I downloaded the mod the Wickeds used to follow us."

"Oh, great. So we're cheating."

"And if we get flagged—and I'm guessing we will if we pull this off—"

"That's pretty much a certainty," said Mansex.

"—then only *my* account will get nuked. The rest of you will be fine."

Mansex nodded. "Works for me. Bandy? Truth?" They both nodded.

A rustle from the woods. <Pwny Xpress> turned to see Yanker emerge from the underbrush.

Boon grinned. "And that's everyone. Let's do this."

<Pwny Xpress> found <Something Wicked> loitering in the final room of the Moonhollow, killing time and the occasional patrol while they waited for the Moon Door to open.

Finding them hadn't been hard. Boon just followed the trail of dead cultists to the circle of stones at the dungeon's end. The Wickeds had been thorough—The Pwnies didn't pass a single patrol on their way in.

Boon peered over a mound of collapsed wall at the horde of Wickeds.

"Looks like they're feeling confident enough not to post sentries," said Mansex.

"Who needs sentries?" said Bandaid. "They've killed everything in the dungeon." Greef was pacing back and forth in front of the dead Wendigo.

Something wasn't right. Yanker spoke up. "Is it just me, or are there way too many Wickeds over there?"

"Shit, she's right," said Mansex. "This is a five-person dungeon, but the Moon was a raid, so you can get fifty toons through an instance for that."

"But that's *more* than a raid," said Bandaid. "There's got to be a hundred players over there."

"More than that," said Mansex. "That's their entire guild."

"Everyone?"

"Yerp. I'm on their guild forums now. The place is a ghost town. Every last member of Something Wicked is here. They're using that cheat mod to follow *themselves* in and bulk up their numbers."

"Right," said Yanker. "We're leaving." She started back down the hall. The rest of the guild trailed after her.

Boon unstealthed in front of Yanker and blocked her path. "Where are you going?"

"Somewhere safe. I don't feel like getting killed and camped today."

"We can still get it back!"

"Look, he stacked the deck, okay? Not even we can fight those numbers. They've got us beat thirty to one. We're a tiny guild. We've got 500 levels to their 15,000 plus. It's suicide."

"Then... we'll get monsters to fight for us!"

"What monsters?" She pointed to the nearest dead patrol. "Those guys? That dead-ass Wendigo? They've wiped the entire dungeon. There's nothing left in here to kite."

"You're right," said Boon. "Nothing in *here*."

"This might not even work," said Yanker. She and Boon peered through the curtain of trees. The great dragon had nearly completed its latest circuit through the glen.

"If it doesn't, I'm out of ideas," said Boon. "You're the genius strategist. I'm scraping the barrel here."

Yanker grunted. She nocked an arrow and took aim at the dragon.

"… Jodie?"

She slackened her grip and glared at him.

"I told you not to call me that." She didn't lower the bow. "I don't *want* to be called that. My name is Yanker. Jodie's pathetic."

"Why do you do that?" asked Reid. "Why do you beat up on yourself?"

"Oh, like you care, now. You wouldn't understand. This is all I get. This is where I'm real. Jodie's life in the meatspace is just baggage."

"You're talking like this is the only place you have any value."

"Sounds right to me." She turned back to the dragon. Her bow arm was shaking.

"But it's not! Most of the people in this game are assholes!"

Now she lowered the bow. "Did you just call me an — ?"

"No! No, just listen to me! Oh, this isn't going well."

"I'll say."

Boon stepped in front of her bow. "What I'm trying to say, is that you don't need the game to be amazing."

"You have no idea who I am." She drew back the arrow.

"You're right!" yelled Boon. "I don't! And I *thought* I did. I actually thought for a while that I was falling for you because I'm so inexperienced at actual human interaction that I can't tell a woman being nice to me from flirting." This *hadn't* been what he was planning to say, but it call came out in a rush. "I don't know, I thought maybe we'd do that bullshit romantic comedy thing where we 'save each other with our magical love' or whatever. But the truth of it is this. You were nice to me, and took me in, and I'm a terrible and selfish little shit who screwed you. And I'm really, truly sorry for that, and I really *want* you to get that meeting with the designers, because if there's *anyone* Boy Howdy needs to hear from about their game, it's their *best. Player.*"

Yanker stared at him. Blankly? Incredulously? It was hard to tell with the game's limited animation trigger sets. "You thought I was *falling for you*?"

"Yeah. And that it was mutual. And we've never even met. Crazy, huh?" He tried not to let his voice shake.

She shrugged. "Not as crazy as this." She fired, and the dragon stormed toward them with a bloodcurdling roar.

Boon fell in to sprint alongside Yanker as they tore back through Inkwood, the enraged dragon at their heels. "You just shot the dragon."

"I totally did," said Yanker. "Never done that before. I've aggroed her a couple times when I got too close, but never intentionally. That was awesome."

"I guess sometimes you have to shoot the dragon."

"Yep. Mind the fire." She jumped and pulled him over a gout of dragon flame that set the woods ablaze. They dove through the black circle an instant before the flames would have hit.

Nothing came through behind them.

Boon and Yanker peered back out the instance. They could see Inkwood swirling there in the inverted colors, but no dragon.

"I don't think she's coming," Boon told Yanker. "She's probably on her way back to the glen by now."

"Doesn't matter," said Yanker.

"Do you want to try again?"

"Nah, not really."

"You won't get the Sword."

She shrugged. "I'm out of ideas. So much for the game's *best player*, eh?"

A scaly tail lashed through the instance and slapped Boon down the corridor. He pulled himself up just in time to see a supremely pissed off dragon squeeze through the instance, shooting fire like a drunken volcano.

Yanker backpedaled past him through the hall, firing ice arrows at the dragon. "I think it worked!" she yelled, and vanished around a corner.

Yanker was taking the long route, leading the dragon around a side loop to the heart of the Moonhollow. Boon sprinted back to the boss chamber—if he hurried, he should be able to beat her there. The rest of the <Pwny Xpress> was waiting.

"It worked, I take it?" asked Bandaid.

"Get ready," he told them. He dropped into stealth and snuck around the corner into the heart of the ruins. Not that he needed to stealth—Wickeds were killing time, with no idea that they'd been followed.

"Just about there," Jodie said in his ear.

Boon ducked behind a pillar. Wickeds milled in the chamber before him. Greef was dancing over the dead Wendigo, bobbing occasionally to teabag it. Standing next to him was Redstar.

❖ ❖ ❖

Reid opened a chat window on his desktop.

CheeZeus: I'm in position. Behind the pillar.

A few seconds later came the reply.

> **RedStar89:** About fucking time.
> **CheeZeus:** Sorry, getting her to come along took some convincing.
> **CheeZeus:** Thanks so much for helping.
> **RedStar89:** Any time. We're on line 4455169.
> **CheeZeus:** Package is almost here.
> **RedStar89:** This had better be awesome.

Reid grinned.

> **CheeZeus:** Oh, it will be. When have I ever let you down?
> **CheeZeus:** Don't answer that.

He switched back to the game.

"Okay," Jodie said in his ear. "Go."

Boon stepped into view, put fingers to his mouth, and whistled. The action broke his stealth.

<Something Wicked> turned his way. Unnoticed by her guildmates, Redstar slipped behind a pillar.

With all eyes on him, Boon gave a wave, stuck his butt in their direction, and slapped it.

The Wickeds raised bows and guns and readied spells. *I certainly hope this works.*

There was a deafening roar behind him. Yanker bounced past just as the Wickeds fired.

Boon dropped into stealth, and Yanker hit the floor. Magic and missiles screamed through where they'd just been and straight into the dragon.

In a millisecond, the dragon had swiveled to target the great-er threat—the guild that just shot it in the face—and belched a river of napalm into their ranks. Burning Wickeds flailed in all directions, setting untouched comrades on fire and perishing before their healers could react.

"Dear God." Mansex's voice was quaking with emotion. "They should have sent a poet."

Boon unstealthed behind his former guildies. "Hold back a tick. Let the dragon do the work."

"You think I want to miss this?" Mansex sounded like he was wiping away tears. "Thank you, Reid. It's perfect. How did you know?"

Greef staggered about in the middle of the chaos, shouting at his guild to fall into ranks.

The dragon slammed her tail to the ground and shattered the floor. The shockwave toppled the nearest standing stones onto the front line of Wickeds. A quick gout of fire took care of any survivors under the stones.

Greef sent the next wave forward. He'd managed to wran-gle his guild back into some semblance of order, and retreated to the rim of the room to direct the battle—which put him just where <Pwny Xpress> was waiting.

"Now," said Boon. "Just like we talked about."

Mansex hit Greef with an ice bolt and froze him in place. Greef whipped out his net. Yanker shot it out of his hand.

Greef glanced over his shoulder at the battle. The dragon was wading through a swath of dead Wickeds, spitting lances of fire at the handful of survivors. The living milled around in chaos; the dead lay in blackened heaps. The dragon pounced on and devoured the survivors one by one.

<Pwny Xpress> surrounded Greef. "You really think this will work?" asked Yanker.

"It might. It was your plan," Boon told her. "We just never got to try in on the First God. Okay, switch to that GroupSpeak line I just chatted you... now."

Horrified frenzied screaming. The dragon crushed a half-dozen Wickeds under her paw and bit the heads of a row of others.

The ice spell was wearing off. Greef would be free to move soon. So Boon stepped in front of him and waved. "Hi! I'm Reid! You know, the guy you lied to and stole the Godsword from? Yeah, I'm gonna need you to go ahead and give me that back."

"Well, balls on fire," said Greef. "So you rolled a new toon, huh? And took him to 100? Too bad the effort's gone to waste. Think I'll hack him and take him sniping in Marrowstone's orphanage."

Redstar slid in front of Greef. "Give him the sword."

"Redstar?" Greef sounded confused. "What are you...? No, don't tell me you're *with* this clown?"

"I'm not with *anyone*. Jesus."

"I got that sword for *you*."

"You got it for *yourself*," she said.

"My God," he spat. "I have done *everything* right. What is it gonna take?"

"Giving the Sword back. You've been using illegal mods and stealing passwords. So it's like this: give him the Sword or we'll report you."

"Try and prove that. I'm an Admin in good standing."

"We've got your computer's IP," said Mansex. "It won't be hard."

"So then I'll hack *your* accounts and delete *your* toons as well. You think I can't find your account holder info? Maybe I'll post some kiddie porn on the Boy Howdy forums under your names while I'm at it. Really?" He laughed at them. "This was your plan? You seriously thought you could blackmail me?"

"Well, no, not really," said Redstar. "But we did think we could get you to admit that shit on air so we could record it, which, yeah, you're gonna want to resign from guildmaster now."

"You cold-hearted bitch."

"The other part was to distract you long enough so the rogue could pick your pocket."

"What?!"

"Got it," said Boon. He ruffled Greef's hair. "Thanks for running interference."

"No prob," said Redstar. "Now if you'll excuse me, there's a dragon killing my guildies." She saluted the Pwnies. "Kill y'all later."

"I like her," said Mansex.

"I *loved* her," muttered Greef.

Redstar ran into the fray, throwing shields and heals at every Wicked in range. It was a doomed charge from the start, and she knew it, and she died bravely alongside her guild.

"That was the greatest gift in the game!" yelled Greef. "I did everything for you! I made this guild what it is! Don't I deserve even a little—!" The dragon swallowed him before he could finish.

"Dragon," said Bandaid. "Might want to hurry."

Boon opened a trade window with Yanker and dropped the Godsword in it. "I believe this is yours."

"You promise not to go crazy and start killing people?"

"*I* make no such promise," said Mansex.

"To be fair," said Reid, "it wasn't me last time."

"*Dragon,*" said Bandaid.

Yanker took hold of the hilt and hefted the Godsword above her head. She was backlit by dragonfire roasting the last of the Wickeds.

With <Something Wicked> dead, true to its programming, the dragon switched to target the next greatest threat in its aggro range: <Pwny Xpress>.

The guild circled up as certain death stormed towards them. Yanker tucked the Godsword away in her inventory.

"Thank you, Reid," said Jodie. "I'm not kissing you."

"Aww," sighed Bandaid. The dragon stomped her into kindling.

"Lame," said Mansex. "Kill me now." The dragon obliged.

The Truth did his tank thing and planted himself before them. He lasted two hits.

"She's so much deadlier up close," said Jodie.

"I never noticed that about her," said Reid.

Yanker looked at Boon out of the corner of her eye. "Hey, Reid… do you want to meet?"

The dragon burned them alive.

15
IRL

TIP: As much fun as this game is, it's just a game.
Be sure to visit your friends in real life as well!

Lodge threaded his sedan between taxis to pull up to the airport curb. Reid popped out and pulled his duffel bag from the trunk.

Lodge leaned out the window. "Are you sure you're ready for this?"

Reid looked up at the international departures sign. "Of course not."

"It's okay if it doesn't work out."

"I know."

"Don't have any expectations."

"I don't."

"And if everything falls apart and you need a place to stay, you're always welcome."

"Thanks, man. I think I would take you up on that this time."

"And if you *do* wind up needing to stay down under for a little while... for whatever reason..."

"Then we'll deal with that if we come to it."

They shook hands. Lodge saluted and drove away.

Thirty hours later, Reid stepped out of customs. He hadn't slept a wink and his body was calling bullshit on it being day outside. The flow of arriving passengers carried him into the airport. He looked around for a person he knew but whose face he didn't.

He saw tanned girls in enormous sunglasses chatting on cell phones; chubby American tourists pointing at koala-themed ads; a pre-verbal toddler shrieking and babbling with delight when his father surged out of the crowd and scooped him up.

Through the stream of bodies, he spotted a young woman standing behind a row of luggage carts, watching the river of people flowing out of customs. She was about Reid's age, and she had the jitteriness of a deer glimpsed on a nature walk, as if she might bolt at any second. Her hair was the same color and thickness of a bale of hay. She'd pulled it back, but it was already tearing its way free, a couple strands sticking up in back like a rooster's comb.

Reid could see a uniform under her peacoat. He chanced a wave.

The pale straw-haired girl blinked at him. She tried a smile on, but it fled.

Reid raised a sign above his head: <Reid>.

She grinned slightly, and raised one of her own: <Jodie>.

Everyone in the airport might as well have vanished. Reid walked her way, halted on the other side of the baggage carts. He didn't want to spook her any more than he already had. "Hi."

Her cheeks flamed. He'd never seen someone blush so hard. Apparently it embarrassed her, because she covered her face with a hand. "Hey."

Reid offered his hand. After a moment, she moved her hand away from her face and took it.

❈ ❈ ❈

Glossary of MMO Pidgin

aggro (ˈagrō) *n.* the range at which a hostile NPC or monster will notice and attack a player. *abbr.* aggression. **draw aggro** *v.* to be noticed and attacked by a hostile NPC or monster.

alt (ôlt) *n.* a player's non-primary character; a secondary character.

bio break (ˈbīō brāk) *n.* a trip to the bathroom.

bot (bät) *n.* an autonomous NPC programmed to respond to a limited range of prompts from players; a robot.

buff (bəf) *n.* a temporary stat boost. *v.* to give a temporary stat boost.

cooldown (ko͞oldoun) *n.* the amount of time that must elapse before an action, ability, or spell can be used again.

DC (dēˈsē) *v.* to disconnect; to be disconnected from. *abbr.* disconnect.

deco (ˈdekō) *n.* non-interactive elements of scenery; decoration.

dot (dät) *n.* a spell or ability that deals damage at regular intervals over a set amount of time. *v.* *[trans.]* to inflict a dot upon. *abbr.* damage over time.

DPS (dēˈpēˈɛs) *n.* the average amount of damage a player deals per second; a character whose role in a group is dealing damage in high amounts. *v.* to deal damage in high amounts. *abbr.* damage per second.

drop (dräp) *n.* a piece of loot in a monster's drop table that has a chance of being "dropped" as treasure when the monster is killed.

drop quest (dräp kwest) *n.* a quest that drops as a piece of treasure from a monster's drop table rather than being given by a quest giver.

drop table (dräp 'tābəl) *n.* the entire range of items a monster could potentially drop as treasure when killed.

elite (ə'lēt) *n.* a monster or NPC three to five times as strong as a regular monster or NPC of the same level. *adj.* three to five times as strong as a regular monster of the same level.

endgame ('end‚gām) *n.* gameplay performed by players who have reached the level cap; *adj.* of or related to the most advanced content currently available.

farm (färm) *v. [trans.]* to search for a specific drop or mat by performing the same tasks over and over, e.g. repeatedly killing a monster, waiting for it to respawn, and killing it again.

gank ('gaNGk) *v. [trans.]* to kill any player that is facing a substantial disadvantage; to kill a single player with a group; to kill as a group. *abbr.* gang kill.

grief ('grēf) *v. [trans.]* to harass or torment.

griefer ('grēfər) *n.* one who griefs.

grind ('grīnd) *v.* to perform an activity over and over again, usually in order to strengthen a character.

guildie ('gildē) *n.* a member of one's guild.

instance ('instəns) *n.* a section of the game world, usually a dungeon, that creates a private copy of itself for any character or group of characters who enter it, such that the players may experience its content without fear of interference; an entrance to a dungeon.

IRL (ī'ä'rel) *abbr.* in real life.

leet (lēt) *adj.* elite.

level cap (ˈlevəl kap) *n.* the highest achievable character level in the game, which can increase when expansions or new content packages are released.

lowbie (lōbē) *n.* a low level character, as opposed to a noob, which is an inexperienced and/or poor player.

macro (ˈmakrō) *n.* a button that plays a preset character animation; a button created by the player that serves as a shortcut for an action or phrase that would normally have to be typed out.

main (mān) *n.* a player's primary character.

mat (mat) *n.* a useable good; an ingredient a character with the proper skills can turn into useable materials such as weapons, armor, and potions. *abbr.* material.

meatspace (mētspās) *n.* the real world; the world outside the game.

mob (mäb) *n.* a cluster of monsters with overlapping aggro ranges.

mod (mäd) *n.* an often illegal modification to the game's engine.

ninja (ˈninjə) *n.* a player who steals treasure that was earned as a team from that player's teammates. *v.* to steal treasure from one's teammates.

noob (noob) *n.* *[pejorative]* an inexperienced or poor player.

NPC (ˈenˈpēˈsē) *n.* a character controlled by the computer. *abbr.* non-player character.

off-heal (ôfˈhēl) *v.* to heal as a secondary function; to serve as a supplementary healer.

power level (ˈpouər ˈlevəl) *v.* to gain experience at a faster rate than the game's content is paced to provide, usually with the assistance of other players.

PVE (ˈpēˈvēˈē) *abbr.* player versus environment.

PVP (ˈpēˈvēˈpē) *abbr.* player versus player.

push-duel (pooSH ˈdooəl) *v.* *[trans.]* to bully a player into dueling.

pwn (pōn) *v. [trans.]* to "own" (informal), i.e. to defeat; to defeat by a wide margin; to humiliate one's opponent.

pwnage (pōnij) *n.* superiority over an opponent; superiority in all metrics for comparison.

quest giver (kwest ˈgivər) *n.* an NPC that gives quests to players.

respawn (rispôn) *v.* to return to life in a preset area after having been killed (NPCs and monsters); to return to existence in a preset area after having been destroyed (structures and deco).

rez (rez) *v.* to return to life. *[trans.]* to resurrect. *abbr.* resurrect.

roll (rōl) *v.* to create a character.

RP (ˈarˈpē) *n.* role-playing; speaking in the voice of one's character. *adj.* of or relating to role-playing. *v.* to speak in the voice of one's character. *abbr.* role-playing.

smuggler (ˈsməglər) *n.* an alt created for the purposes of spying on players of the opposing faction.

spam (spam) *n.* irrelevant messages or advertisements in open chat channels; *v.* to hit a button or use an ability repeatedly.

stealth (stelTH) *n.* a form of limited invisibility that is broken by taking damage or interacting with an object, character, NPC, or monster. *v.* to enter stealth.

tank (taNGk) *n.* a character (usually with strong armor and high hit points) whose role in a group is to shield teammates and occupy attackers while the other group members heal or perform dps. *v.* to serve as a tank.

teep (tēp) *v. [trans.]* to teleport. *abbr.* teleport.

toon (toon) *n.* a player's character.

wipe (wīp) *n.* the death of one's entire group. *v.* to be killed along with one's entire group.

PWNED

The Suppwrters

GUILDMASTER
James a.k.a Über

COMMANDERS
Rob "Lorki" Schimmel
Hawke Robinson
thePaperNinja
The Paynes
0whole1

OFFICERS
Douggie Sharpe
Andrew Obertas
Zombie Orpheus Entertainment
Nancy Vancil

JUNIOR OFFICERS
Alexander John Gordon
Chris & Cisco Piazzo
Mike Ott
Doug Medoff
Melissa Cloud
mike (meski) smith
Dustin "Temig" Kikuchi
Jennifer McCaskill
Craig Andrew Marble
   (dresdencypher)
William Gunderson
Sean Huguenard
Bryce Hlavinka
Elaine Duckworth
David Lars Chamberlain
John O'Toole

VETERANS
Matthew Scoppetta
Todd McKimmey
Leslie Sedlak
Brad Roberts
Dave Carroll

Amanda and Brian
Cook
Andrew Grimberg
The Rival Army
Tara Lynn Bruce
Moritz Schubert
Brian Greer
Bill Helms
David Groveman
Douglas Urquhart
Robert Loper
Helen Brubeck
SaintNicster
Brian "Erev" Hirth
Lane Edgington
Jason, the Most Supremely Humble
Gerald J. Smith
Céline .S. Sauvé
Alexander "Xan" Kashev
Margrethe Flanders
Matt Malinofsky
Chris and Meagan Eller
Brad Gabriel
Arion Hypes
Jacob Spangler
Taia Hartman
Fasulkad, Harper
Josh Receveur
Thomas Gibson and Cathy
   Charbonneau
Crystal Skelton
Rygad
Steve Darveau
Brian Lorenz
Cain Eyebright
Rasmus Durban Jahr
Martin Kümmerling
Anthony "DEG" Wright
Myrddin Starfari
Marcus Johansson

Crystal Bland
Mark Hillsley
Christopher Hensel
K. Jeffery Petersen
D.J. Cole
Robert Wood
Zainah Alrujaib
Brian Harkins

STALWARTS
Seth Davis & Kathy Digby
Karet
Vansau
James & Laura Goodwin
Gordon Duke
Jim Wrench
Steven Mentzel
Lauren Carpenter
Jimmy McMichael
Sean "Twitch" Seymour
Randy Butternubs
Mak Kolybabi
sonofskywalker3
Caroline Wood
Allen W. Shepherd
agent_crux
Erik Brammer
Ray Knoebel
Bradley Paul Foster
Sarah Corn
Evan A Lewis
Arbco the Heretic
Scott Slater
Clansmith
Matthew Chijioke
Paul Dressler
Kristin Brumley
Ergo Ojasoo

TJ Vallance
Karl Riffle
Kelly Sorensen
Sutter
Boxmkr24
Theodore T. Posuniak, II
Kieran Stones
Puma "Pink Pummy" Namanari
Steven T Appleton Jr
Courtney Rayle
Max Beckman-Harned
Jax Mezz
F Schultz
Joseph McMullin
Kenny (Bearmanyeti) Cowan
Justin Larson
John Kuzma
Steven Sullivan
Michael B. Hall
Bob Bosce
Chris Bornt
Samantha Genier
Jabrony
Roger Paulo Soder
Nathan Hartshorn
Sandra"WarKitteh"Phillips
Dustin Roberts
the big void
Dave "Pauper" Woods
David Macdonald
Benjamin Cheek
Geoff Roy
Breahna @ Steve Jackman
Michael "Kaleli" Chovan
Marc Wydler
Kai Schmidt
Matthew Chang
Gregory McCausland

Benjamin Walz
C. Joshua Villines
bdrake
Daniel Johnston
Vamp The Undead
Saenofthedead
Scott Casteel
Jonathan and Dawn Garrison
Brad "Mutato" Wilcox
Russell Johnson
Anna Velcheva
Tara and Thomas
Lawrence E. Wimsatt Jr.
Kit Kindred
Ronny Vikman
Laura!
D.J. Cole
Eric Grant
Shawna Hogan
Andrew & Amanda Numainville
Patrick "Rawtooth" Gingrich
Non-Kosher Ian

FREELANCERS
S Hume
Kevin and Amanda Mickelson
Aly White
Mark Carroll
Di Brown
Lloyd Rasmussen
Brooke Johnson
Joahna Kuiper
Gardner Brenneisen
Daniel Ley
Katy Koenen
Mark Renner
Anthony Barnstable
Nils Bernard

Namocsid
Steve Lord
Kelsa
Trystan Hendricks
Greg Arguello
Jake Bottelberghe
Cassandra Humenuk
Mark Featherston
shenhai
Ryan W. Roberts
Jay Shaffstall
Ray M.
Lucas Bradford
Geoff Turi
Jackus
Karen J. Grant
Eric Moede

JOURNEYMEN
JerSpray
Robert S Roberson Jr
Natalie Listemaa
Alexander Lucard
John Munn
Eileen Webb
Rubiee Tallyn Hayes
Michaela Eaves
Don Early
Daniel Capuzzi
Ralph Sanchez
Matt & Emilie Shimkus
Lee Garvin
Karl Hennon
Jonathan Gronli
Scott Oberlag
Jacob Isaacs
Sarah Palms
Wolfgang Bolz

Sarah Pedersen
Dieter the Bold
Crillitor
Mark Alcocer
Rico Scola
James Worley
Dustin Driver
JD Lyda
Stephenie Sheung
Leesa Hanagan
Heidi W.
Alishia Cameron
James "Doomsayer" Hines
Mark Barnett, Jr
Jamie Linde
KarmaLord
Andrew P.
Francisca Mason
Kelley Marie
Quinlan Schultz
Katie Skovholt
Daniel Jensen
Brent Peters
trit
Andrew Lloyd Walker
Kriispy <3
Alexander "Druki" Sanora
R Hanagan
Miguel Aguado
J.A. Salvaggio II
Amy Gunther
J. Patrick Walker
JR "MANTOS" Santos
Steve Jenness
Jason Glaser
Brakus Blue
Frank Hall
CleverHamster

Darris
Candace Pettit
Harald Demler
Becca Quarles
David Wagaman
Lindsay "strtrkn" Brunetto
Margaret M. St. John
Bill "Shijuro" Hand
Stefan Bold
baw
Rhiannon Rippke-Koch
Chris, Jenny, and Meka Ross
Scott Schwartz (MacLaird)
Wayne J. Rodrique
Jonathan Ball
Mark Woolley
Martin A. Nantus
Gingerdoodles
Dylan Gould
Charles R. Cox
Karl Sears
David Freid
Patrick Ciraco aka Ancientgamer
Kurt Zdanio
Carl Rigney
Jaime S.
Kent Rice
Briahlen LouAva Hand aka
  Lady Aliara
Nadine and Pascal Hecker
Laurel Anne McInnis
Stephen "Stormcaller" Guttridge
Michael Peroutek
Chad Biar
Renee Bell
Az & Red Scott
Robert Drager
Michael G Townsend

RJ Howe
Matthew Topping
Benjamin Goy
Kathleen & Kyle Hunt
Chisholm
Evan Saft
Scott Crespi
David Harriss
Christopher_J_Kemper
James Yoho
Joe Cortese
Rod Meek
Matthew Joseph Longo
T. Rob Brown
Lacwant
David Prasser
PJ Richards
Freekymunky
tilde.d
Mexider
Brian LaShomb
David W. Cooney
Nathe & Alicia Lawver
Douglas Michel
Damon Hammes
Joseph Perez
Anonymous
Brendan Lapsley
Jennifer Duke
Matt Carr
Zinddra
chris eby
Christos Bistis
Toni Siragusa
Sigmundur Mørkøre
　(Mylbp2ps3)
Jesse Sherman
Hal Greenberg

Steve Borne
Robert S Macy
Tina & John Tipton
Terry Sofian
Heath White
Alex A
Andrew Harmon
James McKendrew
Jeffery Murray
Steven Hykes
Lyrania
No, thank you
Nahla Wanless
John Idlor
Chris Volcheck
Michael Feldhusen
The Cooper Clan
Saxon Weber
Tovvok
Sarah Kabli
Jim Vitz
The Brazilian Okapi Guy!
Jeff Gilkison
Ed
Eetu Hellevaara
Jeff DeLeRee
Dominene L. Hernandez
Chris Deutscher
Matthew Guggemos
Robert Hayenga
Michael Daley
Andrew "Rogo" Rogerson
Rob Meyers
Raphael Reitzig
Kyle Hart
Michael C Carter
Ross B.
Andrew & Heather Kalafut

Jan Forslid
J'ohn
Umberto Lenzi
Justin Ashley Powell
Juliet Youngren
Analog Games LLC
Inconsiderate
Brady Friedrich
Nathan "Made of Awesome" Rust
Tom.M.Smith
William Wright
Will Ansell
JacLyn S. Jones
TheRed|Kommie
Kris Leeke
Mark Crocker
Matt (Beek) Buechler
Oswald042661
J Barden
Mernwyn Took
Matt Cardinal
Jeremy Pickard
Chris M
the Dead Gamers Society
Danoumas
T Kampfe
Jordan Hite
Cole
Paul Bean
Jason Gunter
Zackariah "Big Zack" Warren Tegel
Janna
Tyler Leger
Chris Rooney

INITIATES
Rob Hunt director of Standard Action
C. Christian Scott
Cristy Donahue
Matthias
Ben Bernard
Colin O'Kelley
Victoria Masters
Mark The Red, Last of the Blood Fire Berzerkers
John A
Julie Alexander
Shaun D. Burton
Michael Pleier
Houman
Damon Richard
Paul G.
Matthew T. Crawford
H. Anthe Davis
Christopher Peters
tzenes
Yolanda N. Ceron
Anduz
Shaun Johnson
J.D. Dresner
Daniel "Dunec" Provencio
Natasha Ennis
Hannah W
James Neumayer
Tara Imbery
Sandy Holmes
Grace Livingstone
Alicia
Logan Jai Chu
Rachel Grinti
Thomas (Hacksoor) Morton
Lotta & Simon Djerf

Gary Williams
Antonio Rodriguez
Bess Klein
Raanaa
Alison J. McKenzie
Rachel Binfield
Jenny D
Rachel LaFond
George Panopoulos
jerobolod
Beth Perrin
Luke Gaul
Christoph Hardebusch
Tobias B. Peters
Mike Selinker
Brittany Dueker
Seville Duradar
Kevin "Nimmy" Niemczyk
Jason "Stunt Orc" Jenkins
LiQuid!
Jobm
Henrik Warpefelt
Matthew Chan
Kelly Olmstead
Brad Loxley
Harlan & Nanette
Allan Samuelson
Charles and Jessica Stott
Frédéric Fiquet
Leon Higley
Hel Thomson
disposedtrolley
Eat more lentils & kale
Riley Weckbacher-Robeck
Zuhur Abdo
Praxix
Jan Grimmer
Russ & Liz Lambert

Jamie Blakeman
Jeff Prather
Zach Bertram
Andrew Allison
Sean K Reynolds
Roy of the RooSackGamers
TrueWill
Jason F. Broadley
Susan Bischoff
Bryce Vails
jaymi elford
Josh Tobin
Shadowcthuhlu
Steph Goswitz
Scott Gustafson
Glen Roberts
Jenny & Jeremy Engel
Scott Henke
Eric Itow
Donald Milliken
Wrendrak
Mark Moreland
JimTo
David Nielsen
Val Kinman
Jeannie Doege
Sarah A. Gubbins
Charlotte E. English
Brooke "Thumper" Ujvari
Geraldo Macedo
Robert Foose
Jamie Chambers
Winston Crutchfield
Keith Stanley
SunshineGrrrl
Daamon Bintz
Jacinta Colvin
Pamela Lunsford

Michelle Huss
Donovan J. Bertch
Tony Basile
Christopher King
Tommy Foster
Matt
sYa
Sarah Geerling
Manuel Siebert
Ashton War
Paige Barnett
Phil Nicholls
Michael "Maikeruu" Pierno
John E
Joanna Gaskell
Kirk Staley
Kerallyn Thistlehair
Anonymous
Isabell Düwel
Jonny Napalm
Zartan, the anti-Lord of the
    Jungle
eighteyed
Drew Hayes
Jason Lambirth
Xavier Aubuchon-Mendoza
caesar48@gmail.com
Peter Boyen
JiveAlfalfa
Sharlene Glennie
F. Jansegers
Calvin Jones
Josh Straub
Trin Miller
Ray Schmidt
Walter Roadknight Legge
Philip J. Binkowski
Robert Untucht

Eric Feay
Dana Ford
Nikki Jeffries Sørensen
Bruce L. Wehrle
Jeff Hosmer
Craig Duffy
Brenna Lee
every108minutes
Dedstuff
Rudy "Chainsaw" Basso
Kari Parkhurst
Don't put it in, thanks.
undeadkiller0
Gideon
Miles Matton
Alexandre Colaço
DCF
Diana C.
Jed Brooks Smith
Jennifer Corbett
Christopher M. Plambeck
Ted H.
Geraldine Macci
Peredhil
Tanika S. Perryman
Robin
Ray Chiang
Woody Arnold
SwiftOne

About the Author

Matt Vancil is a writer, filmmaker, and game designer based in Seattle. He wrote and directed the *Gamers* movies and created the comedic fantasy series *JourneyQuest*. His narrative work covers feature films and web series, video games and tabletop role-playing games, and live interactive performance. He works for video game studio Z2 and teaches screenwriting at the Seattle Film Institute. A graduate of the American Film Institute, Matt has an MFA in Screenwriting. He lives in Tacoma with his wife and son and misses you terribly.

You can learn more about Matt and his work at his rarely-updated website, www.invancible.com.